ć

... The D........

... — treats its readers to some
...ly comic observation. "Mums are
only like sophisticated computer programs,
after all," Melvin reckons.

The arch-fiend Darius O'Fee, running an
after-hours, fee-paying academy, uses mind-
bending virtual reality techniques to turn
Melvin's schoolmates into goody-goodies.
But Melvin is strengthened by the spiritual
support of a Victorian ghost and a girl who
seems to have a gentle crush on him. Set in
an imaginary town outside Brighton, this
South Downs story is breezy adventure-
writing at its best.

**Michael Thorn**
**Times Educational Supplement**

# THE GENIUS ACADEMY

## Roy Apps

MACDONALD YOUNG BOOKS

*To Peter Hoare*

First published in 1997 by
Andersen Press Limited

This edition published in 1997 by
Macdonald Young Books,
an imprint of Wayland Publishers
61 Western Road
Hove
BN3 1JD

Text © Roy Apps 1997

British Library Cataloguing in Publication Data is available.

ISBN 0 7500 2184 5

Phototypeset by Intype London Ltd
Printed and bound in Great Britain by
The Guernsey Press Co Ltd

Cover illustration © Paul Young 1997

**Melvin**
*and the DEADHEADS*

# I

*There are four of them. Three men and a woman. They sit around the gnarled table in the farmhouse kitchen, stony-faced.*

*'I put the House on the market today,' the woman says.*

*'Angela! You had no right without consulting Guy, Darius or me!'*

*'I agreed to it,' says Darius.*

*'So did I,' says Guy.*

*'So why wasn't I approached?'*

*'After the mess you've made of things, Harry?'*

*'We need the House! How else are we empowered with the strength and the knowledge to carry the deadheading programme through?'*

*'I have made plans to buy it back, under another name, of course,' says Angela, with icy calm.*

*'Little good the House did you or the programme!' mutters Darius, glowering darkly at Harry.*

*'If you think you can do better, why don't you take control of the future programming attempts?' snaps Harry.*

*'I will!' declares Darius. 'If Angela and Guy are agreed.'*

7

*They nod their assent.*

*'I can't believe a mere kid could've fouled it up!'* sighs Harry, visibly shaking with anger and frustration.

*'I can,'* says Guy. *'I see enough of them every day of my working life to believe they are capable of anything.'*

*Darius coughs, discreetly. 'That's why I believe we should forget the adults next time.'*

*The others register the ice-cold smile on his face.*

*'That's why I believe we must deadhead the kids, instead. Every one of them.'*

# 1

## 'The bearded face and shoulder-length hair of an ageing hippy . . .'

For Melvin Perkins, autumn term started as autumn terms always did. His football boots were found in a foul-smelling heap at the back of the hall cupboard, too encrusted with last winter's mud to be of any use. Two whole Saturdays were spent on boring shopping trips into Brighton for new boots, new books, haircuts, sandwich boxes and a leotard (not for Melvin, of course, but his younger sister Ellie). Two whole Sundays it rained.

His first free Saturday, Melvin lay in bed and worked out an agreeable timetable for his morning. It was this: an hour or so on the sofa reading the latest *Lay of the Dork* book: *The Seventeenth Saga, The Raising of the Hare*, then a gentle ride up Hogman's Hill to Hogman's Thorn House to see his friend Arnold Thomas.

Melvin settled himself down on the sofa and studied the cover of *The Raising of the Hare*. Gubbins the Grogg, hero of the Dorks, stood facing the piercing eyes of Furg, the sinister and all-powerful Queen of the Voles. She held a shining sheath knife between her white teeth. He'd read all *The Lay of the Dork* sagas. In fact, they were the only books he ever read.

'Melvin!'

Melvin looked up. And blinked. For a moment, he thought Furg, Queen of the Voles was standing there by the sitting-room door. It wasn't. Though it was something not unlike her: it was his mum. She had her hair tied back into a headscarf and her car keys clasped between her front teeth. Melvin groaned. He just knew what she was going to say. Mums are only like sophisticated computer programmes after all, and on the third Saturday of every month Melvin's mum was programmed to say, 'Don't forget it's your turn with the hoover, Melvin.'

'Don't forget it's your turn with the hoover, Melvin. And you can give me a hand putting the shopping away when we get back.'

She slammed the sitting-room door behind her for good measure. One of her pictures rocked in its frame on the wall.

Melvin's mum had taken up painting during the summer holidays. She had even been to classes at the adult education hut behind the school kitchens. Melvin hoped she might start painting something interesting, like nudes. So far though, she had only painted what she called 'non-figurative', which seemed to mean a lot of blue smudges with yellow blobs ('Landscape With Daffodils') and loads of black smudges with red blobs ('Still Life With Cherries').

Melvin turned back to *The Raising of the Hare*. He began to read. The pages turned slowly at first, then faster. Melvin reached the chapter where Gubbins the Grogg finally gathers his army of dormice about him ready to do battle with the evil Queen Furg of the Voles. Would they be victorious or would the might of the cruel tyrant be too much for them? Melvin was about to find out when the sitting-room door creaked open.

'Melvin . . .?' whined a small voice: Ellie, his younger sister.

'What?'

'Done my painting.'

'Do another. I'm reading.'

'You've got to come and see it!'

'Can't Hannah see it for you?'

'She's *very* busy.'

'Doing what?'

'Her nails.'

With a groan Melvin rolled off the sofa and followed his little sister upstairs to her tiny bedroom. There was a large piece of paper covered in lurid red and purple squiggles on Ellie's table.

'It's Red Riding Hood being eaten by the wolf,' declared Ellie.

'I thought Red Riding Hood gets away?' asked Melvin.

'Not in my picture,' replied Ellie darkly.

As soon as Melvin's mum had been bitten by the

11

'art' bug, Ellie had followed suit. Indeed, one fine day Mrs Perkins had come home to find that Ellie had covered an entire bedroom wall with squiggles, scribbles and doodles. Melvin had got the blame for this, of course: he should've been supervising his little sister. Ellie had run off wailing like a siren. As a peace offering she had been given a frame to put one of her favourite paintings in. For some reason it was no longer hanging above her bed.

He was about to ask Ellie where it had gone when a sound like a prolonged burp wafted up the stairs: the front doorbell. It had stopped going DING! DONG! DING! DONG! years ago. Every time it burped it reminded Melvin that his dad wasn't around, because he knew if his dad had been around, it would've been fixed.

'Hannah! There's someone at the door!' called Melvin.

But nothing stirred in Hannah's room. That was hardly surprising. Being fifteen, she thought it beneath her dignity to perform an act so menial as answering the door when her younger brother was at home.

Melvin went back downstairs.

The Perkins' front door had thick, bubbly coloured glass in it. It made visitors to the house look sort of *melted*, as if they'd been zapped by volcanic ash, like the tribe of giant hedgehogs who try to destroy the kingdom of the Jordiz in *The Uttrin of*

12

*Drivelly* (the seventh *Lay of the Dork* saga).

Melvin opened the door and the melted features transmogrified into the bearded face and shoulder-length hair of an ageing hippy.

'Is your mum in?'

Melvin didn't reply. After all, finding an ageing hippy on your doorstep is one thing; hearing him ask for your mum is quite another.

Melvin grappled with his brain. 'She's popped out to Sainsbury's,' he managed to say.

'Oh. I'll come back in half an hour.'

'Make it two,' advised Melvin, knowing how often his mum got in the One-Basket-&-Cash-Only queue when she had a packed trolley and an Access card.

The ageing hippy was peering hard into the hall.

'I think they're what I've come for,' he announced, pointing to a stack of paintings standing against the hall radiator. 'You know about the Art Competition?'

Everyone in the Perkins' household – even the cat – knew about THE ART COMPETITION. Along with all the other members of the Art Group she had attended over the summer holidays, Mrs Perkins was submitting a stack of paintings to it. The winning pictures were going to be shown at a special exhibition in the Town Hall Art Gallery and there was a prize of £100 for the outright winner. THE ART COMPETITION – and the Art Tutor called 'Gorgeous George' had been Melvin's mum's sole topics of conversation for the last six weeks.

'Yeah . . .'

'Right! I might as well just take them then, shall I?' said the ageing hippy, making his way towards the paintings. Melvin knew his mum was expecting 'Gorgeous George' to pick the paintings up himself.

'Actually, they're going to be picked up by my mum's art tutor . . .'

'I *am* your mum's art tutor!' purred the ageing hippy, stroking his beard.

For the second time in as many minutes, Melvin found himself gawping.

'And you must be . . . Marvin?'

'Melvin.'

'Yes. Kate's told me all about you.' He smiled at Melvin, as if he was party to some dreadful secret.

How could my mum think any ageing hippy 'gorgeous'? thought Melvin.

'Five canvases, I believe?'

Trying to engage his brain again, Melvin counted the paintings. 'Er, there's six actually.'

'Six? Kate has been busy! No problem!' He picked up the pictures, and stumbled out towards the front door, just avoiding tripping head over heels on a discarded skateboard.

It was over an hour later before Melvin's mum got back.

'Honestly, Melvin, why didn't you invite him in

for a coffee or at least do something to keep him here till I got back?' sighed his mum.

'Because,' Melvin replied, 'you told me once never to let strange men into the house.'

'Melvin, he's my art tutor.'

'Art tutor he may be, but he's still a man and a very strange one at that, if you ask me.'

'I didn't ask you, Melvin.'

'I thought he was quite dishy,' cooed Hannah, pulling a copy of *Cosmopolitan* from the shopping.

'How do you know?' asked Melvin.

'Saw him from my bedroom window. I'd definitely take art if he taught at our school.'

'I'm going out.'

'He is definitely your sort, Mum.'

'That's quite enough of that, Hannah!'

Even though it was over five years since his dad had left, Melvin's mum was very touchy on the subject of *other men*. Hannah though, seemed to think it was a great laugh.

'I said I'm going out,' announced Melvin.

'I done eight paintings this morning!'

'Have you, Ellie?'

'I said I'm going out, Mum –'

'Have you heard about the fabulous new Youth Centre they're going to open up, Hannah?'

'I've seen the posters . . .'

Melvin gave up trying to get a response. Instead, he quietly shut the door behind him.

'There's all sorts going on. Sounds the sort of thing you'd do well to get involved with, Melvin, instead of moping about reading. Melvin . . .?'

Melvin was already out of the house, wheeling his bike down the front path. He was going to head out of Smallham towards Hogman's Thorn House. He hoped that when he returned for lunch his mum and sister might have recovered their sanity, but deep down he doubted that such a thing was possible.

# II

Damien Higgins, captain of Sir Norman Burke Middle School football team sticks out his foot. The ball takes a wild ricochet and lands with a thud in the back of the net. Unfortunately for Damien and his team, it's the Norman Burke net.

Esther's ginger moustache bristles with excitement. This isn't because he's watching the school of which he is Head Teacher play a Saturday morning match against St. Philomena's Juniors. After all, it's difficult to get excited about a football match which your school is losing seven-nil. No, Esther's ginger moustache bristles with excitement because of what his suntanned and purple tracksuited guest is explaining to him.

'You see, Mr Ranson, the funds available to the Youth Arts and Sports Trust, combined with our revolutionary training methods, mean that we can turn ordinary ability into exceptional talent. Your football team's striker there – the one who's just tripped over his laces and fallen face first into the mud – a few weekends with us and we could turn him into a British Eric Cantona.'

'Eric who?'

'Think of us as a kind of Genius Academy, Mr Ranson. Whatever the subject – maths, art, music, sport, chess, computer science, we can produce geniuses.'

Esther's moustache bristles some more. He thinks how much he would love to be Head Teacher of a school at the top of the Government league tables. If Smallham's new Youth Arts & Sports Academy could turn out geniuses for him out of school hours, then this could be a reality – and with no cost to the school budget!

'I shall be delighted to publicise your Grand Opening Evening among my staff and pupils, Dr O'Fee.'

'Good!'

'I am sure you'll be able to interest a lot of them – and their parents.'

'I intend to be able to interest all of them!'

Esther's guest beams profusely, but the Head Teacher of Sir Norman Burke Middle School is too busy looking forward to the day when his school will be top of the Government league tables to recognise it for the sinister leer it really is.

## 2

## 'Great instruments of torture . . .!'

Smallham is an ordinary, small town, nestling snugly at the foot of the South Downs. It is in ordinary, small towns, of course, that the most terrifying and inexplicable things happen.

Like finding out that your new friend is a ghost. More precisely, the ghost of a Victorian pickpocket, murdered by his sadistic schoolmaster.

It had been at the beginning of the summer term that Melvin had first met the ghost of Arnold Thomas at Hogman's Thorn House. But now as Melvin sweated and pedalled his way up Hogman's Hill, he realised he'd hardly seen Arnold since the 'For Sale' boards had gone up at Hogman's Thorn House some three months previously.

Not that this was Melvin's fault. For no sooner had the house been up 'For Sale' than it had been 'Sold' and the builders had moved in.

But now, Melvin saw that the renovation of Hogman's Thorn House was complete. Not only that, but the gates were invitingly open.

SMALLHAM YOUTH ARTS & SPORTS
ACADEMY
DIRECTOR: DR DARIUS O'FEE
ACTION! ACTIVITY!! ADVENTURE!!!

screamed a two-metre high hoarding.

Melvin rode in, hid his bike in the shrubs and called out, 'Arnold! Arnold Thomas!'

'Perkins! Perkins! Where have you been?'

Melvin spun round and found himself facing the familiar pale, gaunt face of his ghost-friend. He was still pale, still scruffy, with a filthy mop of brown hair; he was still wearing his collarless shirt and corduroy trousers ripped right up to the knee. But then, of course, ghosts don't have to wash or change their clothes, thought Melvin.

'Had to go to London – to stay with my gran,' he explained.

'For six weeks?'

'No. After that, Mum, Hannah, Ellie and me went to Wales. On holiday.'

'Oh I say, quite the Grand Tour,' muttered Arnold.

'I did come up here once or twice . . .'

'And tore off again mighty fast!'

Melvin sighed. Of all the ghosts in all the world, why was it he had to meet one who whinged so much?

'Would you have hung about, with a dozen beefy

builders all waving shovels at you?'

'I have to hang about. I have no choice. For over a hundred years I've been tramping these grounds . . .'

'Yes,' sighed Melvin. 'I know.' He guessed what was coming next.

'And I am condemned to do so until my murder is avenged.'

Melvin groaned. 'Arnold, I still can't see how I can avenge your murder when it happened a hundred years ago . . .'

'It has to be done! Otherwise I am condemned to haunt these grounds for all eternity!'

'How?' Melvin was half beginning to wish he'd not bothered to come, but even the company of a whingeing ghost is preferable to the company of a whingeing fifteen-year-old sister, which is what Melvin would have faced at home.

'I wish I knew for sure,' said Arnold. 'But there must be connections. The past and the present aren't separate worlds, Perkins. They are enjoined by a thousand threads.'

'I'll try and help,' said Melvin, though there was no sense of optimism in his voice.

'You're a true friend,' said Arnold. He shook Melvin's hand. It felt to Melvin like brushing against a bubble; there was nothing of substance save a faint clamminess.

Ghost and boy sat propped up either side of a silver birch tree in silence. Then Arnold nodded in the direction of the house.

'As a true friend,' Arnold went on, 'and in the name of humanity, I suppose I should warn you.'

Melvin's heart missed a beat. 'Warn me of what?'

'Of the hideous sights now to be found within the House.'

'What hideous sights?'

'They have been filling the rooms with great instruments of torture!'

'Torture . . .?'

'Yes. The leather strap that was used so abominably while I was a pupil in that place is nothing, compared with what is now being planned for some poor unfortunate souls.'

'What kind of instruments of torture?'

'Come! I will show you.'

Arnold glided through the undergrowth and Melvin crashed after him.

When they came out into the large, sweeping frontage of the house, Melvin was surprised to see how bright and even welcoming the renovated building looked. Gleaming white paint shone on the windowframes, boxes of scarlet geraniums trailed from the window-sills. It was difficult to believe that barely three months before, Harry Summerskill and his sinister colleagues from WhoppaShoppa UK had used this place as a studio to produce subliminal images for videos that turned most of the adult population of Smallham into unthinking, unseeing zombies – deadheads.

'They've certainly cheered the place up a bit,' said Melvin.

'It's what they've put inside that will chill your bones to the marrow,' warned Arnold.

They made their way to a large downstairs window.

'Take a look in there, if you think you've a constitution strong enough to stand it,' said Arnold.

Melvin flattened his nose against the cold windowpane.

'See that rack? A favourite device of the Spanish Inquisition!' declared Arnold excitedly.

'Arnold . . .'

'And those weights . . .? Used for pressing witches, they were.'

'What?'

'They used to place them on a witch until her rib cage started to crush and she began to confess . . .'

'Arnold . . .'

'And those ropes! Death by slow hanging!'

'Arnold! This room is not a torture chamber – not in the sense you mean anyway.'

'Then what is it?'

'A gymnasium. People will climb those wall bars, lift those weights and swing on those ropes for physical exercise.'

'Of their own free will?'

'Yes.'

23

Arnold shook his head incredulously. 'What an extraordinary notion.'

Melvin nodded. Then he looked through the window again at the gym equipment. 'Hang on . . .! This stuff isn't for grown-ups. Look, that's not a full size exercise bike. And those wall bars are quite narrow. This stuff's for kids!'

'You mean it's going to become a school again?'

Melvin shrugged. 'I don't know . . .'

He ran round to the other side of the house. Arnold followed. Through the window Melvin could make out a semi-circular stage, lights and speakers. 'This is some sort of drama studio. Hey, if this place is going to be a school, it's going to be better equipped than Norman Burke is. Bet it's going to be private.'

Melvin turned away from the house. He still couldn't quite forget what had happened on his very first visit to Hogman's Thorn House just a few months previously, when he had nearly been set upon by a savage dog. He made his way back to the gates.

'Private school or public, I'll wager any sum it'll be a force for evil,' said Arnold, darkly.

'Why? You told me yourself, the forces in this place can be turned to *good* as well as evil.'

'I warrant no good ever came out of any school,' muttered Arnold.

Melvin nodded. He was inclined to agree with his

friend. He knew though, that his experience of Sir Norman Burke Middle School was nothing compared to Arnold's memories of Flogmore Hall. If you had watched your classmates being systematically flogged and had then been murdered by your head teacher like Arnold had, you probably would have a bit of a downer on schools, he reckoned.

They reached Melvin's bike.

And that was when Melvin heard the squeal of brakes and the screech of rubber on tarmac. That was when the white blur sped through the gates towards him. He dived into the bushes, but even so the vehicle passed close enough for him to feel its airstream whistle across the back of his head.

Melvin untwined himself from the bushes. Arnold was nowhere to be seen. But the vehicle that had almost done for Melvin had stopped a little way up the drive. A white Range Rover, he noted.

Out of the driver's door stepped a purple tracksuit. Out of the tracksuit beamed a bronzed and rugged face.

'Hi there!' smiled the face. 'Good news travels quickly, heh?'

Melvin stared at the face blankly. He was aware of an overpowering scent of aftershave.

The Range Rover driver thrust a dazzling dayglo leaflet into Melvin's hand.

'I've only just picked up these from the printers!'

*Smallham's new Youth Arts & Sports Academy!!!*
*A whole exciting new range of after-school,*
*weekend and holiday activities!!!*
*Starting here from the second week of September*
*onwards!!!*
*Yes, you too can be a genius!!!*

Melvin read.

'How does that grab you, heh?'

'Er . . . great,' lied Melvin, who thought it all sounded unnecessarily energetic. Then a small line on the bottom of the leaflet caught his eye. *The Lay of the Dork Simulated Adventure Game!*

'What's this?' he asked. 'This *Lay of the Dork* game?'

'Ah, so you're a fan, are you?'

'I've read all the books.' Truth be told, Melvin considered himself the World's Number One Expert on *The Lay of the Dork Saga*.

'We're devising a simulation game, based on the latest virtual reality technology. . .'

'Wow!' Melvin hadn't meant to sound so excited; but he was, so he did. Out of the corner of his eye he saw Arnold hopping about like a small boy who needs the toilet.

'Perkins! Perkins!'

'I take it I can look forward to seeing you at our grand enrolment evening next Tuesday, then?'

'Yeah,' said Melvin. He pedalled off out of the

26

grounds of Hogman's Thorn House, excited by the prospect of *The Lay of the Dork Simulated Adventure Game* and determined to get to his friend Pravi's place to tell him the great news (Pravi was the World's Number Two Expert on *The Lay of the Dork Saga*). So excited was he that he failed to hear Arnold's frantic calling of his name and failed too to see the hunched figure in reflective glasses in the Range Rover's passenger seat.

# III

*In the grounds of Hogman's Thorn House, two men look up at a fine oak tree that grows just beyond the boundary wall, but whose branches overhang it.*

*The former Chairman of WhoppaShoppa UK takes off his reflective glasses. 'That's where they got in. Climbed up it from the woods, then out along the branch. I'd have it down if I were you, Darius.'*

*'But then, I'm not you, am I, Harry?' shrugs his companion in the purple tracksuit. 'No . . . it can stay.'*

*'Look, Darius. I don't know the exact nature of the technology you intend to use in this programme . . .'*

*'The best.'*

*'It'll need to be. Take it from me, kids breaking in and nosing around can mess an awful lot of stuff up.' He pauses. 'I wasn't going to tell you this, but that kid you caught snooping around the drive just now . . .'*

*'Another potential client, Harry . . .' There is a chilling brightness about his eyes. 'Another potential deadhead . . .'*

*'He was one of the kids who messed up the first programme, I'm sure of it.'*

'Then let him come along to nice Uncle Darius' Arts & Sports Academy. I want them all in here, every one of them.' Darius' lips curl into a thin-lipped smile. 'Yes, Darius wants them all for his stun beam.'

# 3

## 'Perkins! I'm warning you! Keep clear of it . . . .!'

It had once been the Flogmore School refectory, where daily beatings had been carried out on Arnold Thomas and his friends. It had then become the sumptuous dining room for Hogman's Thorn House. It was now the dance and drama studio of the brand new Smallham Youth Arts & Sports Academy and it was full to bursting with Sir Norman Burke Middle School students and their parents.

The newly-polished woodwork shone; the bright red curtains glowed in the autumn evening sunshine; vases of chrysanthemums dotted the window-sills. There was a buzz of excitement in the air.

Onto the stage bounded a pair of Reebok trainers Melvin had last seen leaping out of a white Range Rover. Above the trainers a purple tracksuit. Above the tracksuit a bronzed and rugged smile.

'It really is most gratifying to see so many of you here this evening,' Dr Darius O'Fee began. 'Thank you all for coming.'

Melvin was rather taken in by that touch. *I've been to school about three million times and not once has Esther ever thanked me for being there,* he thought ruefully.

'Looking around me tonight at this sea of young faces,' Darius O'Fee continued, 'I see potential; unfulfilled potential. I see a generation of geniuses.'

Melvin looked round and saw Cassandra Washbone scowling, Jodie Jenkins blowing gum and Damien Higgins yawning.

'Some of you already know about our Youth Arts & Sports Academy, a facility for young people that has recently been set up here by the Youth Arts & Sports Academy Trust. We boast first-class recreational and educational resources that can be put at the disposal of *your* child! I can promise to realise your child's maximum potential,' he continued. 'Yes, all your hopes and aspirations for your child can be totally fulfilled!' He paused and his eyes swept in a great arc across the hall. His voice dropped to little more than a whisper, 'I can nurture the genius within *your* child!'

Melvin looked around. Cassandra Washbone, Damien Higgins and Jodie Jenkins all stared up at the ceiling, bored silly. But their parents were listening in rapt attention.

Darius O'Fee's gushing enthusiasm didn't waver for a moment. 'At the Youth Arts & Sports Academy, we have first-class facilities for sport, art, computer technology, drama, dance, chess . . .' he continued.

Melvin looked around again. Now Damien, Jodie

31

and Kayleigh were as wide-eyed as their parents.

'Membership of our Youth Arts & Sports Academy is open to your sons and daughters for an initial registration fee of five pounds. Once a member, your child will have the opportunity to take part in residential weekends, holiday programmes and after-school events all personally tailored towards your child's particular area of interest.' He paused. 'Don't you owe it to your son or daughter to give them this unique chance to become world-beaters in their chosen field of endeavour . . .?'

The Sir Norman Burke parents obviously did, for Darius O'Fee had hardly sat down, before he was swarmed by hordes of them waving crisp five-pound notes. Melvin's excited classmates discussed which activities they would do. Whatever their interests, somehow he seemed to have an activity starting up that would be just for them. Melvin saw his friend Pravi with his dad.

'May the trusty stave of the Brummis protect you!' Pravi yelled. This was the sort of thing *Lay of the Dork* experts were always saying to each other.

'I take it you'd like me to fork out five pounds so that you and Pravi can wander about bawling out nonsense at each other?' sighed Melvin's mum.

'Please, Mum!'

Mrs Perkins sighed. 'Oh well, perhaps you might learn something enriching and fulfilling and useful here . . .'

'What do you mean?'

'Like . . . I don't know . . . painting for example.'

Melvin groaned. 'Boring.'

'We could become a family of painters, travelling the countryside in a gypsy caravan . . .'

Ever since his dad had left home, just after Ellie had been born, Melvin's mum had always had these dreams. There had been plans for a self-sufficient smallholding in Wales, a pottery in Devon, a Buddhist retreat in Norfolk and a tea room on the Outer Hebrides.

'Mum!'

'Well, Ellie's a keen painter . . .'

'Ellie's six!'

'And I think Hannah is quite artistic . . .'

'Mum, the only thing Hannah's interested in painting is her nails!'

Melvin and his mum joined the queue at Darius O'Fee's desk. When it came to their turn, he burst out with a loud laugh, 'Ah! The *Lay of the Dork* fan!'

Melvin grinned sheepishly.

Darius O'Fee turned to Melvin's mum and smiled her a smile as bright and as broad as a game show host's.

'And ideally, what would you like your son to be, Mrs Perkins?'

Oh no, here we go with the gypsy caravan,

33

thought Melvin.

'That he should be happy and fulfilled in whatever he chooses to do in life,' said Mrs Perkins, somewhat primly.

'But surely . . . you must have other ambitions for him?'

'I don't think so,' said Mrs Perkins.

Melvin thought he saw Darius O'Fee flinch, ever so slightly.

'You wouldn't want him to be more obedient, less obstreperous, more dutiful?'

Mrs Perkins shrugged. 'Twelve-year-olds are twelve-year-olds, Mr O'Fee, you must know that!'

'So he's the perfect son, is he?' Melvin watched the broad smile sour into the faintest of smirks.

'He has his moments,' laughed Mrs Perkins.

Thanks, Mum, thought Melvin.

'But I wouldn't wish him to be any other way.'

Thanks, Mum, thought Melvin again and this time he meant it.

'We open on Saturday evening,' said Darius O'Fee. 'I look forward to seeing you then. Details of our half-term weekend residential courses will be available shortly.' He had been badly rattled by something Mrs Perkins had said, Melvin could see that, even if his mum couldn't.

As they left the drama studio, Melvin saw Cassandra Washbone and her parents sitting down in front of Darius O'Fee. Since the WhoppaShoppa affair, Melvin had hardly spoken to Cassandra. She had taken up her position of class P.W.S.T. (Person What Spells Trouble) with even greater vigilance than before. A mere two weeks into a new term it may have been, but she had already been placed on report for tipping plaster of Paris into Miss Bounderby's cake mix. Even now, when everybody else in the room was bubbling with excitement and enthusiasm, Cassandra was not a happy person.

'And what particular activity would you like to enrol for, Cassandra?' asked Darius O'Fee, flashing his teeth in another broad smile.

'Advanced Level Eco-terrorism,' snarled Cassandra.

'Cassandra!' trilled Councillor Mrs Washbone in appalled tones. Her dad just covered his face in his hands, in a futile attempt to hide his embarrassment.

'Come along, dear,' said Mrs Perkins. She hauled Melvin quickly to the door as if she was afraid that the sight of a snarling Cassandra Washbone could inflict irreparable emotional damage on him.

'Ideally, what would you like your daughter to be, Mrs Washbone?' they heard Darius O'Fee asking as they left the room.

'She might be a long time answering that one,' muttered Mrs Perkins. 'That girl of hers is practically out of control.'

It didn't often happen, but for once, Melvin found himself agreeing with his mum.

They had a look round. The upstairs rooms were all locked, but through the glass doors they could see computers and video equipment.

'Must have cost something,' mused Mrs Perkins.

Downstairs, the gym was full to bursting with screaming sports freaks clambering up bars, lifting weights, beating punchballs. Outdoors on the floodlit football pitch thirty boys who all thought of themselves as potential Man United trialists kicked the fury out of a football and each other.

It was while they were making their way back to the car, that Melvin heard a voice in his ear.

'Perkins!'

He had been on edge all evening, wondering when Arnold would put in an appearance.

'Perkins! I've got to talk to you!'

'Not now, Arnold!' whispered Melvin.

'Sorry, dear?'

'Nothing, Mum.'

'Perkins! I'm warning you! Keep clear of it! This place is nothing more than a *school*! A *school*! And another thing . . .'

Melvin didn't hear what the other thing was. He'd already got in the car and had shut the door. Outside he could see Arnold waving his arms in the air and shouting.

Mrs Perkins eased the car down the drive.

'You're quiet, dear . . .?'

'I was just thinking . . . about that place . . . It's

36

called an Academy. It's not just another *school*, is it?'

'Of course not, dear! You can choose exactly what you want to do there. It's just that you're going to become very good at it! Whether it's sport or music or . . . painting.'

'Mum . . .!'

'Goodness, Melvin, I wish I'd had something like that to join when I was your age. All we ever had was . . .'

'A weekend camping with the Guides at Bognor. Yes, Mum. You've told me before. Many times.'

Yes, Arnold was over-reacting, Melvin thought. Darius O'Fee *was* using the power of Hogman's Thorn House for good. And he had to admit it, playing *The Lay of the Dork Simulated Adventure Game* sounded the best way to spend an evening – every evening – that he could think of.

# *IV*

*There are neat piles of five-pound notes on the desk.
A greedy smile crosses Darius O'Fee's face. A sudden
noise behind him makes him start. He swings round.*

'Harry? How did you get here?'

'I drove.'

'I didn't hear anything.'

'It's surprising what sounds the trees and bushes
in the grounds can hide. Believe me, I should know.'

'I trust you weren't seen.'

'It's dusk. Or haven't you noticed?'

*Darius doesn't reply.*

'How did it all go?'

'You're desperate for something to go wrong,
aren't you, Harry?'

'I merely ask . . .'

'Listen, the deadheading experiment is something
much, much bigger than your bitter and twisted
desire to see me fail in my efforts to get it all started.
I shall not be making the same mistakes that you did
with the subliminal imaging technology.'

'I admire your self-confidence, Darius. But
remember, it comes in part from the power of this
place and of our shared past with it. As such, it may*

give you the strength, knowledge and energy to carry out your programme. But power can also deceive you into thinking that you are untouchable. Things can go wrong, Darius.'

'But so far, they haven't. Everything has gone according to plan. The programme starts this weekend.'

The red curtains shift, seemingly in the late evening breeze. Darius and Harry shiver involuntarily for a moment.

'Only the wind, Harry.'

'If you say so, Darius, if you say so.'

Neither of them can see the ghostly outline of a Victorian urchin boy by the curtain. They cannot hear him, either.

Not when he screams at them, 'You . . . you! Murderous TEACHERS!'

Nor when he whispers sadly, 'Oh, Perkins, my friend. Whatever will become of you?'

# 4

## *'Too* weird . . .!'

'We can't go away tonight, Mum.'

'It's your gran's sixtieth birthday.'

'It's the opening night at the Genius Academy.'

'The Genius Academy is going to be open every night. Your gran's sixtieth birthday is only going to happen once. And she needs cheering up. It sounded on the phone as if she's got a stinking cold.'

A weekend stuck in Gran's poky house in Lewisham. A Saturday and a Sunday when the new Youth Arts & Sports Academy was opening its doors for the first time and *The Lay of the Dork Simulated Adventure Game* was waiting to be played.

To make his feelings known, Melvin said nothing at all during the journey home.

On Monday morning, Melvin trudged up the school path, well loaded down. Not only had he got all the usual stuff in his bag, but there was a history project (1st period), the ingredients for wholemeal scones (2nd period), swimming things (3rd and 4th periods) as well as three hundred and thirteen pages of *The*

*Raising of the Hare.*

He knew the zip on his bag was dodgy. But he thought it would last – at least until he got to his tutor group room. Not even Melvin Perkins, who had constructed Perkins' First Law of Survival (Keep Your Head Down) as a fortress against the harsh cruelties of existence, believed life could be *that* cruel.

But, of course, it could.

As he reached the battered front doors of Sir Norman Burke Middle School, he glanced round and caught sight of Cassandra Washbone stomping along in his wake, just a few paces behind him. Instinctively, Melvin tugged his bag more tightly over his shoulder so that he could quicken his pace down the corridor.

It was a fatal move. The teeth of the zip sprang open in a great ugly laugh and Melvin's project, scone mix, *The Raising of the Hare* all spewed out onto the floor. Before he even had time to swear, Cassandra was at his side. Melvin cringed, wondering what she was going to do. Stamp his scone mix all over *The Raising of the Hare*? Run off with his swimming trunks? Guffaw merrily at his Paddington Bear keyring? His Paddington Bear keyring! No one, not even Melvin's friend Pravi, knew that he kept a Paddington Bear keyring in his bag. His dad had given it to him on his first day at Infant School. It was his lucky mascot. Though,

41

given the kind of luck Melvin was always having, it would probably have been more accurate to describe it as his *un*lucky mascot. Cassandra bent down and pushed her dark hair back from her face.

'Do you want a hand with your stuff?' Quickly Melvin tried to work out what the catch was.

'Clear off, Washbone!'

She didn't clear off. She just smiled some more and started collecting up the various bits of Melvin's history project. He supposed that this was a good thing, in a way; at least the howling hordes of Sir Norman Burke pupils charging through the main doors gave his scattered belongings a pretty wide berth once they saw Cassandra Washbone.

'Open your bag up then!'

'Eh? Oh.'

Melvin opened his bag and Cassandra poured his history project back in.

'You'd best carry it, rather than sling it over your shoulder.'

'Er . . . yeah . . .'

She started walking along the corridor towards the tutor room, then stopped and tossed her head back over her shoulder.

'You coming?'

She was serious.

'Er . . . yeah . . .'

Melvin tried walking two or three steps behind her, just to let everyone know she wasn't really with

42

him, but she kept stopping and waiting for him to catch her up. There had to be a pay off for her somewhere, Melvin thought. Perhaps she would try and tip the bag off his shoulder, or something moronic like that.

'Didn't see you at the Genius Academy on Saturday,' she said.

Melvin looked the other way to try and make out that Cassandra was talking to someone – anyone – else.

'I was in London,' said Melvin flatly. He was aware of people staring at him – or to be more precise, people staring at him talking to Cassandra.

Cassandra's keen hazel eyes darted back and forth. For a moment, the corridor was quiet.

'I need to talk to you! It's urgent!'

Melvin walked on. Been there, done that, he thought. Cassandra Washbone, class P.W.S.T., was famous for 'needing to talk to you'. Then she blew gum in your face, stamped on your toes or snipped off your tie with a pair of nail scissors. Melvin had seen it all. He hurried along to the tutor group room, Cassandra racing along beside him.

He tumbled through the door with Cassandra more or less at his side. A great 'Wer-hay!' went up from all the people sitting on the window side (the boys) and a long, low snigger went up from all the people sitting on the other side of the room (the girls).

'Got yourself a girlfriend, Perky?'

'Aren't you going to sit next to her, Perky?'

It was probably a good job there weren't any mirrors in 8GG's tutor group room. At least Melvin couldn't see how red he was about the cheeks. Then he thought: that's what this is all leading up to! She's going to embarrass me in front of the class! Any moment now, she's going to say, 'Perky's got a Paddington Bear keyring!'

But the strange thing was, she didn't. Cassandra Washbone, class P.W.S.T., wasn't jeering or joining in with the general merriment at Melvin's expense. Nor did she go and sit at the back, next to her hard henchwomen Jodie Jenkins and Kayleigh Foster. Instead she sat right in the front at the KKs' (Keen Kiddies') desk.

Looks were shared and nudges exchanged. Nobody ever sat at the KKs' desk, least of all Cassandra Washbone. But there she was, quietly opening her bag and checking the contents of her pencil case.

In first period, it got even weirder. When the twitchy student teacher tried to encourage 8GG to put up their hands, everyone waited for Cassandra to yell out, 'Where?' but she didn't. She raised her hand right up above her head instead and answered the question.

At morning break, Cassandra picked no fights, wrote no graffiti, scrounged no crisps. She simply wandered about the playground trying to engage her wary classmates in harmless conversation and, or so it seemed to Melvin, constantly trying to catch his eye.

Melvin stuck close to Pravi. Well, that was what friends were for, he reckoned, to keep you out of the clutches of the class P.W.S.T. Pravi was busy enthusing about Saturday night at the Arts & Sports Academy.

'Coke's only 20p you know.'

'What about *The Lay of the Dork Simulated Adventure Game*? What's it like?'

'Didn't get a go,' Pravi sighed. 'You needed this special equipment. It's a bit like a Virtual Reality thing . . .'

'Wow!'

'Yes, wow! Everybody wanted to use it, of course. But only one person got the chance.'

'Who?'

'Who do you think? The person who screamed, shouted, bullied, threatened, pushed and shoved her ugly face to the front of the queue.'

'The Washbone.'

'You *are* sharp,' said Pravi sarcastically.

'You know she told Darius O'Fee she wanted to learn Advanced Level Eco-terrorism?'

They could see Cassandra looking their way.

'She's not behaving like an Eco anything at the moment,' observed Pravi. 'More like a clap-happy

45

Christian. What *is* going on with her?'

'I don't know,' Melvin shrugged. 'But I don't like it. I think I preferred her the way she was. At least you knew where you stood.'

'Yeah, usually as far away from her as possible,' agreed Pravi.

It continued like this all day.

After the last lesson (music), Melvin and Pravi were collecting up *Sixteen Sea Shanties for Schools* for the Leek (Mr Rhys-Williams: Expressive Arts). They were the only other two people in the room when Cassandra went up to him.

'Ah yes, Cassandra . . . now what did I ask to see you for today? Was it insolence, or indolence . . .?' The Leek's memory was going. The poor old boy was really ancient. So ancient in fact that he had taught Damien Higgins' mum *Sixteen Sea Shanties for Schools* back in the days when Sir Norman Burke Middle School had been Tannery Lane Secondary Modern.

'Actually, Sir, I've tried to be well-behaved today and I've sung everything you asked us to,' the Washbone beamed at him.

'Yes . . . you have!' The Leek's wince showed that he, too, preferred things as they used to be, when the Washbone would sit in a sullen silence for the whole of the lesson. The reason for this was simple. When she sang, the Washbone sounded like a cat who has had its tail trodden on.

'Er . . . you're not feeling under the weather or anything, are you?' asked the Leek, in puzzled tones.

'Oh no, Sir!' smiled the Washbone.

'Well then, you can go,' said the Leek.

'You don't understand, Sir. I've got something to ask you.'

'You have?'

'Yes.'

The Leek was absent-mindedly carrying a set of cymbals towards the cupboard. The Washbone chose this moment to drop her bombshell.

'I'd like to join the school choir please, Sir.'

Melvin saw the Leek's legs shake a little as the cymbals tottered in his arms.

Perhaps Cassandra didn't really know what she was doing. She chattered on merrily, 'Dr O'Fee – at the Genius Academy – has arranged for me to have extra singing lessons. You see, Mummy and Daddy want me to become an opera singer.'

Five pairs of cymbals rolled out of the Leek's hands. They clattered their way to the floor, spinning madly and crashing off chairs and tables as if they, too, couldn't stand the thought of the Washbone becoming an opera singer.

Melvin's mum was always going on at him about how he should be kind to old people, but judging by the look of horror on the Leek's face as he stood rigid in the middle of the music room, surrounded by clanging cymbals, Melvin reckoned he was well past receiving any kind of help. He gave Pravi a nudge and they hoofed it out of the Expressive Arts block as fast as they could.

'This is getting *too* weird,' said Pravi as they made their way out round the back of the school. 'I mean it's not natural.'

He was right, of course. Here was Cassandra Washbone, the class P.W.S.T., who had once defined music as what comes out of the mouth of a cow with stomach ache, calmly asking if she could join the school choir as it would help with her ambition to become an opera singer.

'What do you think she's playing at, Pravi? I mean she's putting it all on, isn't she? There must be some purpose to it.'

Pravi was thoughtful. 'I think there's a simple explanation,' he said nonchalantly. 'I think she's in *lurve*...!'

'The Washbone? Don't talk daft. In *lurve* with who?'

'Don't you mean with *whom*?'

'Eh?'

'Don't you even listen to anything we're told in English?'

'No,' said Melvin.

'Put it this way, judging by the way the Washbone's waving like fury in our direction, I reckon you could be the lucky man – Aaargh!'

48

Pravi howled as Melvin suddenly grabbed his neck in an armlock. Well, there are some things that are just *too* serious to joke about.

'May your pathetic body rot in the Myriad Mires of Mansittey!' growled Melvin, quoting his favourite curse from *The Raising of the Hare.*

He and Pravi were approaching the school gate, but they still heard the raucous voice some fifty metres behind them:

'Melvin! Wait for me!'

Instinctively, Melvin dropped his armlock and swung round to see Cassandra waving frantically at him.

'Told you!' said Pravi.

You'd better believe it: the sight of Cassandra Washbone, yelling your name at the top of her voice and beating a path towards you, is an awesome one indeed.

Melvin tore off out of the school gates, Pravi close on his heels. Up Tannery Lane they ran and into the High Street. Melvin was already coughing.

'You'll never make it to your place,' panted Pravi, 'you'd best come and hide in the shop.'

Into Pravi's parents' shop they charged, under the counter and through to the back. Mrs Patel just had time to ask,

'Pravikumar? What are you doing?'

'Sanctuary! Sanctuary!' howled Pravi.

They sat in Pravi's tiny bedroom, sipping Coke,

crunching crisps and quizzing each other on the characters and events, worlds, other worlds and nether worlds in *The Lay of The Dork Saga*.

'Darius promised me that we'll be able to play *The Lay of the Dork Simulated Adventure Game* tonight,' said Pravi excitedly.

'Great!'

'Don't say anything to my dad though,' said Pravi.

'Why?'

'He's not a *Lay of the Dork* fan. He wants me to become a Champion Arm Wrestler.'

'Parents!'

'That's nothing. My mum wants me to do extra maths up there.'

'Why? You're already brill at maths.'

'Not brill enough for my mum's liking. She wants me to take my GCSE in June.'

'But you're only just thirteen!'

'You know my mum.'

'My mum wants me to do painting.'

'You? You don't know one end of a brush from the other.'

'Thanks, pal. No, painting's her big thing at the moment.'

'Take it from me: we're playing *The Lay of the Dork Simulated Adventure Game* all evening.'

After an hour or so, they both reckoned it would be safe for Melvin to venture forth onto the streets of Smallham.

Nevertheless, their eyes still scoured the High Street both ways in case the Washbone was skulking in a shop doorway or behind the bus shelter.

'Can't see her,' said Pravi. 'She'd have to fancy you something rotten to wait around for over an hour for you.'

Melvin nodded, glumly.

'See you at the Academy tonight?'

'You bet! Atchoo!'

'May the trusty stave of the Brummis protect you!' whispered Pravi.

'It's only a cold! Got it from my gran I expect.'

'It's not the cold you need saving from: it's the Washbone . . .'

Melvin caught his friend's eye. There was a definite twinkle in it. 'You're enjoying this, aren't you, Pravi Patel?'

Pravi face fell in mock horror. 'I'm simply concerned for your well-being, friend!'

'You're a sadist,' grunted Melvin, trudging up the High Street towards home.

# V

*There are four of them. Three men and a woman. They sit around the gnarled table in the farmhouse kitchen. The woman and two of the men are stony-faced; the fourth man – the youngest – has a calm smile playing about his mouth.*

*'I am pleased to say that all is going to plan.'*

*The woman raises her eyebrows. 'The children are impressed by your set-up?'*

*'Of course they are, Angie.' He turns to one of his colleagues. 'I'm sure Guy will confirm that.'*

*'They talk of nothing else,' agrees Guy.*

*'Okay, so the kids have fallen for it, but what about the parents?' It is Harry Summerskill, the former Chairman of WhoppaShoppa UK, who speaks.*

*'They will be even happier than the children.'*

*Harry Summerskill doesn't look impressed. 'Won't they soon start asking questions? When they notice their precious little darlings changing before their very eyes?'*

*'When that happens,' replies Darius with supreme self-confidence, 'the only question they'll have is, can't my little darling visit your wonderful centre more often, Dr O'Fee?'*

'I'll believe that when I see it,' snorts Harry Summerskill. The scars left by his own failure at the hands of the people of Smallham have not yet healed.

Darius O'Fee clears his throat and lowers his voice a tone. 'You already can see it, Harry. I was going to save this news for later, but I might as well report that I've already run one child through the programme, both to her and her parents' complete satisfaction.

Darius O'Fee allows a frisson of excitement to pass between the others, before adding, 'And I intend to run as many of the others as I can through it tonight.'

# 5

## 'Arm wrestling with a kipper...'

The Perkins' front door slammed shut.

'Is that you, Melvin?'

'Hang on, I'll just check . . .' Melvin put on a silly voice. *'Are you Melvin? Yes, I am.* Yeah, it is, Mum.'

Mrs Perkins charged through from the kitchen. 'You're late.'

'I've been at Pravi's.'

'You should've rung.'

'Yes, Mum . . .'

'You had a visitor.'

Melvin's heart skipped a beat. He only ever had one visitor – Pravi. And he'd been with Pravi. No, it couldn't be . . . it *had* to be.

'Councillor Washbone's girl.'

It was.

'What did she want?'

'You.' Mrs Perkins searched her son's face for clues. 'I didn't know you two were . . . friends.'

'We're not!' replied Melvin vehemently.

'I know I shouldn't interfere in your private life, Melvin, but I must say she was extremely pleasant.'

'Mum! You know what she's like! You saw her at the Youth Academy last week.'

'That was last week. It already seems to have had a beneficial effect on her. I hope the place will teach you to become as well-mannered and polite as Cassandra, Melvin.'

'You won't have to wait long to find out, I'm going up there after tea. Atchoo!'

'Not with that cold you're not.'

'Mum! It's noth – atchoo!'

The front doorbell burped suddenly.

'Aren't you going to answer it?'

'Me?'

'Well, I expect it's for you.'

'Mum! You never!'

'I told her to call back later, yes.'

The doorbell burped again.

'But I don't want to see her!'

'That's for you to tell her, dear, not me.'

'Ho hum, young love,' muttered Hannah darkly.

'Mum! I've got a cold! You said!'

But Mrs Perkins had already disappeared up the stairs with what she considered to be great tact. Melvin slouched through to the hall. One mauve and one green eye peered through the other side of the glass in the door. Even though it was distorted through the mottled glass, Melvin recognised the long dark hair. He opened the front door.

'Melvin, I need to talk . . .'

'Yeah, but I don't need to listen.'

'But, Melvin, it's important . . .'

Before Melvin knew it, Cassandra Washbone had grabbed his hand. She squeezed it hard. Melvin flinched and pulled away.

'Leave off, Washbone! Atchoo-o-o-o!'

Cassandra leapt back from Melvin's megasneeze. Which just gave him time to slam the front door well and truly shut.


Wednesday evening, Mrs Perkins said, 'I think you'll be well enough for school tomorrow.'

Melvin said: 'Then I'm well enough to go up to the Genius Academy tonight.'

Dusk is a sudden affair in this part of the country as the evening sun drops suddenly behind the South Downs. By the time Melvin reached Hogman's Thorn House, the dense trees and shrubs of the front gardens were but dark grey shadows merging into the night sky. Only the bushes nearest the drive showed any sense of form, lit up by a curving line of knee-high lights there to lead people safely to the front door of the Academy. A jumbo jet rumbled overhead, flashing its wing lights. Then it was gone and all was quiet.

Suddenly a pale form seemed to be blocking Melvin's path.

'Perkins? Is that you?' Arnold spoke in a hesitant whisper.

''Course it is.'

Melvin peered into the darkness.

'Can you see me?'

'Just.'

'I have dreadful news.'

A car tooted on its way up to the house. Melvin recognised Sarah's dad's Volvo.

'You are the only one who can save them.' Arnold sounded weary, desperate, frightened even.

'Save who?'

'Your friends.' Melvin could just make out Arnold's pale shape looking in the direction of the Academy.

'They are in there, being made to do all kinds of hideous things. Climbing bars like monkeys . . .'

'Gym, yes . . .'

'Having a large ball thrown at their heads!'

'Football practice, yes . . .'

'Hurling themselves about the floor as if they are in the final throes of some hideously painful disease . . .'

'Dance, yes. I told you, Arnold, strange though it might seem to a Victorian like yourself, modern kids do these things of their own free will.'

'Are you sure?'

'Of course! Arnold, you've just got this thing about schools. I can understand why, seeing as you were tortured and murdered by a teacher, but believe me this place is okay. Does it look evil?'

Warm lights glowed from every window in the Academy; bright music could be heard; there was laughter and gossip as people chatted on the doorstep.

'Those aren't the screams of kids being tortured, or beaten.'

They were right by the front door now.

Arnold shrank back. 'Don't go in, Perkins! I beg of you!'

Melvin propped his bike against the wall and walked into the Academy.

The place was buzzing with Sir Norman Burke pupils.

'Hi, Melvin!'

'Hi, Melvin!'

'Hi, Melvin!'

Melvin had never been greeted in such a friendly manner before. He peered through the door into the drama studio. A group of boys and girls were dancing. Melvin noticed with a start that one of them was Damien Higgins. Then he realised with even more of a start that they were ballroom dancing.

But it just puzzled him; that was all.

He came to the end of the corridor. Outside at the back of the house, on the all-weather pitch, he saw Sarah dribbling a football through a series of traffic cones. Some girls lived for football he knew, but he knew also that Sarah wasn't one of them. Now her little brother Jamie, that was another matter. He had been football crazy. That's how he had got knocked down and killed. Running into the road after a football.

It puzzled him some more, that was all.

'Melvin! I thought you were never coming!'

Melvin spun round and saw Pravi beckoning to him.

'Fancy a game?'

'You bet!' said Melvin.

He followed Pravi into the coffee bar area.

'Where's the equipment then?'

'Equipment?'

'You can't play a *Lay of the Dork Simulated Adventure Game* without simulation equipment, can you?'

'*Lay of the Dork . . .?*'

Melvin sat down opposite his best friend. Pravi put his elbow on the table.

'Best of five.'

'Eh?'

'I should warn you. I am good. I am going to be a World Youth Champion Arm Wrestler.'

'Pravi? What about *The Lay of the Dork*?'

Suddenly, Pravi gripped Melvin's hand and forced it down onto the table with a thud. 'It's what my father wishes.'

Pravi gripped Melvin's hand in his again, and for the first time Melvin realised how *cold* his friend's hand was. It was like arm wrestling with a kipper. Melvin's knuckles hit the table once more.

'Three more. Then I must go. Darius is setting me some maths. I shall take my GCSE in the summer. It's what my mother wants.'

'You what?'

'Melvin! At last! No doubt you would like me to show you our *Lay of the Dork Simulated Adventure Game.*'

Melvin looked up into the fixed smile spread across Darius O'Fee's face.

'It's upstairs at the back of the house.'

Melvin followed Darius O'Fee up the broad staircase. At the top, someone stood blocking their way. Someone Darius O'Fee couldn't see.

'Perkins! You must go back!'

Melvin stopped on the stairs. For no other reason than that he felt it would somehow be creepy to walk *through* his friend.

'Him. I have seen him before.'

Melvin felt his mouth drying up.

'I saw him here. Back in the summer. Watching the moving picture machines. With Harry Summerskill. He was part of WhoppaShoppa UK. Go, Perkins! Before you're deadheaded like the rest of them!'

'Is something wrong, Melvin?'

Melvin looked into the leering face. He remembered, with a sickening lump in his throat, Harry Summerskill's face, as he had stood in the school hall, planning to deadhead the members of the

Smallham Says NO To Shopping-centre Campaign.

He turned and ran down the staircase.

Without looking back, he sped down the corridor and straight out of the front door. Then he was onto his bike and away, the chill October air stinging his tear-stained cheeks as he pedalled for all he was worth down the drive.

He didn't stop pedalling until he reached home.

He told his mum he wanted an early night if he was going to school in the morning. That pleased her.

Not that he could get to sleep. When he did eventually doze off, it was into troubled snatches of nightmare: he was by a river with his mum and Hannah and Ellie. They were all painting pictures. But every time Melvin put his brush on the paper, it became a portrait of Darius O'Fee's smirk. A smirk that widened and widened until Melvin was swallowed whole by it.

# VI

As he steps into the farmhouse kitchen, he sees that the other three are waiting for him.

'Everything okay, Darius?' asks the woman.

'Fine!' says Darius. But there's an edge to his voice that gives him away.

'There's something wrong, isn't there?' Harry Summerskill's accusation is quick and sharp.

'I had another half a dozen through the programme tonight. They're happy. Their parents are happy. And why shouldn't they be? We're doing them a favour. Giving them the sons and the daughters they want.'

He doesn't mention the boy. There is no way he is going to make Harry Summerskill's day by mentioning a little problem called Melvin Perkins. He is Darius O'Fee after all. He has the knowledge, the power. He has the ultimate in deadheading technology at his fingertips.

'Harry. Watch my lips. Everyone is happy!'

Watch Darius O'Fee's lips. See them curl into a thin leer.

Other people's happiness is the last thing on his mind.

# 6

## 'Aie-ee!!! I'm going to be hung!'

Melvin was woken by a piercing scream.

'Aie-eee!!!'

It came from downstairs. It came from his mum.

'Aie-ee!!! I'm going to be hung!'

Melvin grabbed Hannah's hockey stick and charged down the stairs.

Melvin's mum was dancing around the hall, waving a letter. But there was no sign of a rope round her neck.

'Look, Melvin!' Melvin's mum shoved the letter in front of his nose. '*Dear Ms Perkins*,' the letter read. '*We are pleased to inform you that your painting entitled UNTITLED has been selected to be hung at the Town Hall Art Gallery as one of the finalists in the Open Art Competition. We look forward to seeing you at the Prizegiving and Preview Evening at the Gallery. Please find free tickets for family and friends as requested.*'

'That's great, Mum!' sighed Melvin.

She gave Melvin a kiss, then stepped back. 'Melvin. Why are you holding Hannah's hockey stick above your head as if you're about to try to club me to death?'

'Er . . . because . . .'

Hannah ambled down the stairs and took the letter about the Art Competition out of her mum's hands. 'Which one was UNTITLED?'

'Mmm, I don't know . . .' Mrs Perkins frowned. 'They all *had* titles. I imagine what's happened is that the label on the back's come unstuck. It's probably "Still Life with Cherries". That one's certainly my best.'

She was so busy with spreading the good news – first she rang 'Gorgeous George', then her friend Debbie, then Melvin's gran – that by the time she got to the rest of the post, Melvin was just about to leave for school.

'There's a letter for you, Melvin!'

A mail-merged label on a buff envelope. Inside was an orange day-glo leaflet.

*Special Half-term Events at The Youth Arts &*
*Sports Academy!!!*

it announced. There was to be a special weekend residential event followed by 'a performance of talents to all parents on Sunday evening'.

The previous evening's events surged through Melvin's mind again. He felt sick. He screwed the leaflet up into a tight ball and hurled it at the rubbish bin. And missed. Immediately the leaflet unfurled itself. Mrs Perkins bent her head to one side and read it.

'They're even offering art sessions!' She sighed.

'I can't fork out twenty-five pounds; not just at the moment . . .'

'But, Mum, I don't want to go!'

Melvin's mum sighed again. 'Believe me, I'd quite happily pay twenty-five pounds for a weekend for you at the Genius Academy, if I had it, Melvin. But I haven't.'

'Mum. I don't want to go!' muttered Melvin vehemently.


School was worse.

It was like being in a class full of strangers. Jodie Jenkins, Queen of Techno Music, smiled at him sweetly at break. She held her Walkman to her ears.

'Would you like a listen?' she asked Melvin.

Melvin shrugged. Jodie Jenkins had never spoken to him before.

He put the headphones to his ears. Whoever it was, it wasn't a techno music band.

'Who's the singer?'

'Cliff Richard. I'm a big fan!'

'You're not. . .!'

'I am!'

'Why?' It seemed the obvious question.

'It's what my mother wishes.' It seemed the obvious answer.

The rest of the day continued in much the same vein. Melvin kept out of Cassandra's way – not that there was anything unusual about that. He also kept clear of Pravi and Sarah. Not that they sought him out. Together with the rest of the class, they were busily discussing the forthcoming exciting residential weekend at the Genius Academy.

At lunch time, Melvin sat alone amongst the graffiti on the wall by the old bike shed. He felt as if he was in a dream. Everyone else was a player; but he was just a spectator. Once he went up to Sarah as she kicked a football against the playground wall.

'Going to play for Arsenal?'

'It's what my father wants,' she said.

It wasn't what her father really wanted, Melvin knew. It was what he had wanted for Sarah's little brother Jamie. He was trying to turn Sarah into Jamie.

For now, everyone was happy, particularly Esther, and the rest of the teachers and parents. But it couldn't last, Melvin knew. For it wasn't just their parents and teachers whom his friends were so ready to obey unquestioningly, it was Darius O'Fee himself, too. One night, everyone's mums and dads would roll up at the Genius Academy to collect their children and find the place empty. Darius would have gone; Pravi, Sarah, Damien, Jodie, even the Washbone would have gone with him to do whatever he wanted them to do.

Leave them to it, Melvin thought. Perkins' First Law of Survival – Keep Your Head Down. But he found his First Law of Survival to be of little comfort. He was deeply troubled by the dreadful knowledge that he had. It was even worse having no one with whom he could share it. Of the small group who had known about and fought the original deadheading programme, Pravi, Sarah and Cassandra were all deadheads now. There was Cassandra's brother, Bunny . . . surely he would have noticed something? And there was Hannah . . .

As soon as he heard Hannah come in from school, Melvin charged across the landing to her room.

'Hannah?'

'What.'

'I want to ask you something.'

'The door's open.'

Hannah's walls were covered in posters of sad-eyed, fresh-faced, pouting boy singers. Hannah herself sat up in her bed reading one of their mum's old copies of *Cosmopolitan*.

'Hannah . . . you remember the deadheading business?'

'Yeah.'

'Do you think they'll come back?'

'Why should they?'

'To have another go at their deadheading programme, of course.'

'What are you on about?'

'Hannah . . . They're back. They're running this

"Genius" Academy place. The Director bloke was involved with WhoppaShoppa UK.'

'How do you know?'

Melvin paused. Then replied quietly, 'Arnold.'

'Arnold . . .?'

'He's just a . . . friend.'

No way was Melvin even going to attempt to explain to his cynical sister that Arnold was the ghost of a Victorian pickpocket who had been murdered by his head teacher.

'Does he go to Sir Norman Burke?'

'No! Listen, Hannah, it's true! Darius O'Fee is out to deadhead every kid in Smallham!'

'And how does he intend to do that?'

'I don't know exactly, but . . .'

'But your friend Arnold said . . .'

'Pravi's been done – and Sarah. Pravi's into extra maths. He looked blank when I mentioned *The Lay of the Dork*.'

'Perhaps,' said Hannah, acidly, 'he's growing up.'

'Sarah thinks she wants to be a footballer . . .'

'Girls can play football, you know, you sexist pig.'

'I know. But not Sarah! She's not a sporty-type.'

'Don't you think people's mums and dads are going to notice? I mean *we* noticed, didn't we, when it happened to our parents?'

'Don't you understand, Hannah? They're being deadheaded into the kind of people their parents want them to be!'

68

'Melvin. The only kid in this town with a dead head is you. Here, you haven't been drinking or anything, have you?'

'No!' yelled Melvin indignantly.

'Perhaps it's those *Lay of the Dork* books you've always got your head in, turning your brain funny. If you've got a brain . . .'

'Hasn't Bunny said anything to you about Cassandra?'

Melvin should have seen his sister bridle, but he didn't.

'I don't know anyone called Bunny,' she said icily.

'All right then, Warren . . .'

'I don't know anyone called Warren, either.'

''Course you do! Cassandra's brother – your boyfriend!'

'I haven't got a boyfriend.'

'Yes you have!'

'Little brother dear, boys are of no interest to me. I have my GCSEs, my future career to think about. Now why don't you toddle off to your bedroom like a good little boy?'

Only then did Melvin tumble. Bunny had chucked Hannah.

No Pravi; no Sarah; no Bunny and no Hannah. Arnold was right. Melvin was on his own.

# VII

*He sits in a book-lined office. It is quiet now. The children are still at home. They haven't yet come out to play and the Genius Academy doesn't open for another half an hour. He holds a bright red pencil in his hand and studies the two lists of names in front of him:* The Smallham Youth Arts & Sports Academy: Members. *All the names have a little \* against them except one: Perkins, Melvin Lloyd.*

*He squeezes his fist. The bright red pencil snaps in two.*

*'Your time will come, sunshine,' he mutters to himself.*

*A sudden draught leads him to think the window might somehow be open. He gets up to see to it, but finds it is shut fast. It is then there is a knock on the door.*

*'Come!' he calls.*

*A woman enters. She is large, smiling and she carries herself in the manner of one who knows her own importance.*

*'Councillor Washbone! An unexpected pleasure!'*

*'Forgive me dropping by like this, Dr O'Fee, only I wanted a word with you before tonight's Council*

*meeting . . .'*

'Not at all, dear lady. I hope there is no problem with Cassandra . . .'

'Good gracious no! Quite the opposite. She is a different girl since she started coming here!'

'Good! That's the idea.'

'She'll be along to see you later . . .'

'Good.'

'She can't wait to start singing lessons . . . she's joined the school choir. And her personality is so much better. She's lost that edge. In fact, it's true to say that every parent I've spoken to is absolutely thrilled by the work you're doing with our young people.'

The smirk is as wide as a game show host's. 'So kind of you . . .'

'That's why I'm here actually. As you are quite the flavour of the moment in the town, I wonder whether you would consider performing a little ceremony for the Council at the Town Hall?'

'I'd be delighted! Precisely what little ceremony are you thinking of . . .?'

# 7

## 'On the dark side of the house . . .'

'Are you going up to the Academy tonight?'
Melvin's mum asked him after tea on Thursday.

'I doubt it. He thinks he'll be brainwashed,' said
Hannah, with a mischievous smile.

Melvin glowered at his older sister.

'What's a brain wash?' asked Ellie.

'He thinks Pravi's been brainwashed, because
he's started doing extra maths apparently,' said
Hannah.

'Good for him,' said Melvin's mum. 'I think
they're doing marvellous work. Look how the
Washbone girl has changed.'

'Yes, she's taken a shine to Melvin,' said Hannah.
'Highly bizarre behaviour.'

Melvin glowered at her again.

'Hannah, that's enough.'

Enough? Too much at least, thought Melvin.

He stomped out, unable to control his anger or
his tears. His friends were being systematically
deadheaded at the Youth Arts & Sports Academy
and everybody apart from him seemed to think it
was a good thing. His mum's total lack of under-
standing, Hannah's sarcasm – he couldn't stand it

any longer.

He cycled away from Hogman's Hill out towards the river. He watched the sun disappear behind the great looming hills. Then everything turned as dark as he felt. He would have liked to visit Arnold, but he dared not venture into the grounds of the Genius Academy. Sooner or later he knew, Darius O'Fee would be after him and he didn't know what to do. The mere thought of it made him want to move on; go back home; hide.

He heard the van coming up behind him as he pedalled up the deserted High Street. He saw it overtake. Then it stopped at the pelican crossing outside the Co-op. Melvin stopped behind it.

Too late did he realise that there was no one on the crossing. Too late did something in his brain tell him to get going. As sharp as a rifle shot, the back doors of the van swung open. Melvin's bike was kicked from under him and he fell into a pair of arms which immediately threw him into the back of the van. His bike followed after him. Then the doors clanged shut. He grovelled about in the pitch black, stumbled to his feet, then was thrown against the side of the van as it roared off. He was going to die. He knew it.

A bright torchlight shone in his face. He blinked. Then blinked again as its owner yelled above the deafening rattle of the engine: 'Hi, Melvin!'

Cassandra Washbone.

Now he knew the truth. He *wasn't* going to die. No, it was worse than that. He was going to the Genius Academy to be deadheaded.

Suddenly the van screeched to a halt and Melvin was thrown back again. He heard the driver's door slam. Then the back doors opened.

'Hi, Melvin!'

Bunny.

'You're going to sit in the front. With Cas. It's the ride from hell sitting in the back and I don't want you throwing up over my mate's van.'

Melvin climbed into the cab. Cassandra squashed up beside him. Her long hair brushed the side of his face.

'It's all right. I'm not going to jump on you,' she said. She seemed to be back to her usual, rude, aggressive self.

Bunny turned the ignition and they were off again. Not up the hill towards the Genius Academy, but down towards the bypass.

'Where are we going?' yelled Melvin.

'Brighton,' yelled back Cassandra.

It was difficult to talk in the cab, so noisy and distracting were the vibrations from the engine. It had started to rain and the windscreen wipers scratched and squawked like a couple of argumentative crows. Bunny peered intently through the windscreen. They were following the coast road. Past the aggregate works and the D.I.Y. Superstores, past the harbour and the yacht club they drove, on along the wide, windswept Hove seafront and into Brighton proper.

The lights of the Palace Pier sparkled through the rain. Bunny turned off the seafront and eased the van down a narrow side street. He bumped it up onto the kerb and switched off the engine. Melvin's ears still sang and his shoulder ached where he had been thrown against the back of the van. He wanted to go home.

'All change!' announced Bunny.

Bunny and Cassandra led Melvin out of the van and through the front door of a decaying, bow-fronted terraced house.

'Sorry. Hall lights aren't working. Someone's nicked the bulbs,' sighed Bunny apologetically. 'The bannister's to your left.'

'Where are we going?' asked Melvin, for the second time.

'Room 101,' hissed Cassandra with a wicked glint in her eye.

'My flat,' said Bunny.

The stairs creaked and sagged alarmingly. All the way to the top of the house they went.

Bunny's room was large, but there wasn't a lot in it. A mattress (no bed); an old table and chair, a pair of dirty socks and a stunning music centre. The frayed curtains appeared to be nailed to the wall. Bunny ushered Melvin to a space on the floor.

'Why have you brought me here?'

'Couldn't talk at Mum and Dad's now, could we?' explained Bunny.

'Couldn't we?' asked Melvin.

'She's not a problem; it's a Council meeting tonight, but Dad's due back from London this evening,' Cassandra said, by way of explanation.

'Not too bruised, are you? Sorry we had to pick you up like that,' said Bunny.

'It's his own fault,' snorted Cassandra. She pushed her hair back from her face. 'I tried to talk to you enough times, you grade one thickhead, didn't I? Before school; during school; after school. I even went to your house! You ran a mile each time! Hey, you didn't think I fancied you or anything, did you?'

'No!' lied Melvin. Yet despite his embarrassment and his anger, a wave of relief swept over him. Cassandra was back to her normal P.W.S.T. self.

'I thought you'd been deadheaded.'

'Ah. So you know they're back. I rather guessed you might,' said Bunny.

'But I'm not one of them!' snapped Cassandra. 'No one, not even suntanned, leering owners of Genius Academies with stupid names deadhead Cas Washbone.'

Her brother cast her a reproving glance.

'Well . . . not for long, at any rate,' added Cassandra, a trifle sulkily. 'It's the strength of my mind, see . . .'

76

'It was something more than that,' said Bunny.

'Excuse me,' Melvin interrupted, 'have you dragged me all the way here just so that I can listen to you arguing?'

'Sorry,' said Bunny. 'I'll make some coffee.'

'I don't want coffee,' said Melvin, annoyed, 'I want some answers.'

Cas and Bunny looked startled. Melvin's tone was firm, uncompromising. The power to say what he really thought that had arisen in him after his very first visits to Hogman's Thorn House, had returned.

Bunny went over to a small, grubby, hand basin and filled a kettle.

'If you just stop interrupting, I'll explain,' said Cassandra.

'I'm not interrupting – '

'There you go again!'

Melvin opened his mouth to speak, then closed it again quickly.

'That first weekend at the Youth Arts & Sports Academy – what a stupid name – '

'Get on with it.'

'Don't interrupt! That first weekend . . . Darius O'Fee told me I could become a wonderful diva.'

'A what?'

'An opera star, bird brain. Anyway, I told him he was a few quavers short of a crotchet.'

'And what did he say to that?'

77

'He told me I could have a go at the new virtual reality game that the centre had got.'

'So you did?'

Cassandra nodded. 'It's at the back of the house, upstairs. Well away from the rest of the stuff . . .'

'On the dark side of the house . . .' murmured Melvin. 'Where the sun never shines. The evil side.'

'Don't interrupt! There's a huge helmet thing you put over your head, a bit like one of those huge hairdryers old ladies wear at the hairdresser's when they have a set.'

'I don't suppose Melvin has ever had a set,' smiled Bunny, placing three chipped mugs of grey liquid on the floor between them. 'Coffee.'

Cassandra ignored her brother. 'There are a pair of gauntlets and boots too.'

'What was it like?'

Cassandra seemed to be thinking hard and Melvin realised that for once, incredible though it seemed, the class P.W.S.T. was lost for words.

But not for long.

'This is the strange thing. It wasn't wow-fantastic-exciting or anything like that. . . . It was just *real*. There were tastes, smells, sounds – all very real.'

'But what were the tastes and smells of? What did you see? Do?'

'I can't remember.'

'Cassandra!'

Bunny grinned ruefully.

78

'I think I was singing,' said Cassandra with a frown.

Melvin shuddered at the horrific thought.

'Anyway, when O'Fee took the helmet and stuff away – '

'You'd changed,' Melvin suggested.

'No! *I* hadn't changed. The world had.'

'But you had changed!' Melvin protested. 'You were all smiles that Monday morning. You told the Leek you wanted to become an opera singer.'

'That was an act,' said Cassandra. 'The world had changed back again by then.'

'Eh?'

'I went to my cousin Claire's birthday party on the Sunday. And while I was there, all of a sudden the real world – my old world – started to come back.'

Melvin shot Cassandra a look.

'And before you say anything, no, it wasn't anything I drank or took. It wasn't that sort of a party. My aunt and uncle were there for goodness' sake.'

'And when the world changed back, all that opera singing stuff, was that still there?'

'In my head, yes. But it was like I had dreamt it. Yeah, it was like I'd had a very vivid dream. Now being sharp and intelligent . . .'

Bunny and Melvin both groaned and Cassandra beamed in appreciation.

'. . . I realised that O'Fee's VR game had done

something to me – turned me into a doting, dutiful daughter no less – and that the only way to find out exactly what he was up to, the only way to make sure he didn't try to deadhead me again was to pretend to still be part of his world, all goody-goody, wanting to become an opera singer – '

' "Because that's what my parents wish me to be," ' intoned Melvin.

'You're interrupting again, but as I've finished anyway, I won't thump your head in,' said Cassandra benignly.

'You're so kind.'

'Then she rang me,' said Bunny. 'I made some investigations at the University, about the latest developments in VR, that sort of thing . . .'

'And . . .?'

'Think for a moment about what is real. Is it the physical world – or the world that exists inside our heads?'

'Our imaginations, you mean?'

'Not so much our imaginations as our dreams.'

'Who's to say that our dreams aren't the real world and the other stuff – our day-to-day experience – isn't just fantasy . . . make believe?'

Melvin's most common, recurrent dream sprang across his mind with all the force of a bolt of lightning:

*He comes downstairs. There is a purple and green melted face peering through the glass of the front*

80

*door. He opens the door. He looks at the face, briefly. It's his dad come back. Then the face melts into purple and green. He wakes up.*

In many ways, Melvin knew, there was nothing more terrifying, more haunting, more real than that nightmare. But Bunny had taken a sip of coffee and was hurrying on.

'In our physical, everyday world we hear, touch, smell and taste – that's why it's physical. In dreams though, you can't touch, taste or smell anything. But – '

'Are you listening, Melvin?' asked Cassandra, abruptly.

'Of course I am!'

'Good. Because it's important.'

'But supposing,' Bunny managed to say at last, 'supposing the technology is available to alter that? Remember the subliminal imaging technique the deadheaders used before? Look how well that worked – and that was only visual stimulus. Imagine an experience that seems to take place inside your head, an implanted dream, if you like, that you can not only see, but touch, taste, smell, hear. Do you know what happens? That becomes your reality.'

'And what about your everyday life. Your *real* reality, if you see what I mean?'

Cassandra answered Melvin's question. 'Take it from me. It goes on. But you experience it, like you experience dreams.'

'The important thing is, that it's the other reality that you start to live,' added Bunny.

'That's what happened to me,' said Cassandra. Her dark eyes flashed with anger. 'And that's what's happened to Sarah, Pravi and all the others. They've been deadheaded into the kind of . . . of . . . *creatures* . . .'

Melvin shuddered at the word.

'. . . their parents want them to be.'

'Mum always wanted to be a singer,' said Bunny. 'But she never got farther than the Smallham Amateur Operatics. She's forever on at Cas to take singing lessons.'

'And while you were deadheaded, you really wanted to become an opera singer?'

'Not really wanted, exactly,' said Cassandra thoughtfully. 'More like a dull feeling that this was what I had to do.'

Melvin shuddered again and remembered the mechanical tone of Pravi's announcement that he was going to become World Arm Wrestling Champion.

'*It's what my father wishes.*'

'And Darius O'Fee doesn't suspect that you're not a deadhead any more?'

Cassandra shook her head. 'Thanks to my brilliant acting skills.'

There was a moment's silence. Then Melvin asked quietly, 'So why tell me all this?'

'For a start, you're not a deadhead,' said Bunny.

'How do you know I'm not?'

'I checked,' smiled Cassandra.

'Checked?'

'This particular VR process would seem to lower the victim's body temperature slightly,' explained Bunny, 'just like when you're asleep, so that your hands tend to feel cold and clammy.'

Melvin remembered his arm wrestling bout with Pravi.

'Remember I grabbed your hand – when I came to your house?'

Melvin remembered – and felt his cheeks prickling with embarrassment.

'I was checking. To see if you'd been deadheaded or not.' Cassandra paused. 'You really did think I fancied you, didn't you?' she guffawed.

Bunny ignored his younger sister's merriment. '. . . And not being a deadhead means two things. One: you – and Cas – are the only people who can stop Darius O'Fee's deadheading programme.'

'How?'

'Oh, I'll think of something.' Bunny wanted to sound convincing, but he didn't. He added, under his breath, 'If Cas could think what it might've been at Claire's party that turned her back, it would be a help.'

'Well, I can't!' snapped Cassandra.

'What's the second thing about not being a deadhead?' asked Melvin.

'That's obvious, isn't it?'

Melvin's blank look showed that it wasn't.

'You're in pretty deep doo-dah. Darius O'Fee is desperate for your head. Desperate. That's why we thought it was important for you to know that you've got friends.'

Melvin caught Cassandra's eye. She pulled a face.

'If things get too much, there's always a place here for you to stay,' said Bunny.

Melvin glanced around at the Spartan room. 'Thanks.'

'I'd better get you two back to Smallham.'

Nobody said anything on the drive through the rain home. It wasn't just the noise of the engine, either. The seriousness of the situation was making itself felt on all of them. Despite all her bluster, Cas was frightened. She wasn't very confident she could keep up her pretence of being a deadhead for much longer. Bunny felt desperate – he had no idea how to tackle the deadheads this time round. And Melvin . . .? Melvin just felt numb.

They dropped him off at the bypass roundabout, 'It's best if you make your own way home from here,' Bunny said. 'We can't be too careful. We'll meet you here at half seven tomorrow evening.'

'Aren't you meant to be on the residential thing at the Genius Academy?' Melvin asked Cassandra.

'They think – and so do Mum and Dad – that my big brother is taking me to the opera – very important for my career. I'm not going up there until first thing Saturday morning.'

'If your friends are to be saved, we've got to act quickly,' said Bunny.

'But we don't even know where to start!' retorted Melvin glumly.

'Get thinking then, bird brain,' snapped Cassandra.

# VIII

'Darius! It's him! Getting his bike out of that crate of a van!'

'Who?'

'Perkins!'

'Are you sure, Guy?'

'For goodness' sake, man, I see him every day of my working life, don't I?'

'Did he see us?'

'No . . . no. I'm sure he didn't.'

'Who was he with?'

'No idea.'

There is a squeal of brakes as Darius O'Fee throws the Range Rover into a U-turn.

'What are you doing, man, trying to get us both killed?' Guy looks genuinely frightened.

'I'm trying to get Perkins!'

The Range Rover heads off the roundabout onto the narrow winding incline of a road that leads into Smallham. There is no sign of the van, but a small, wet figure can be seen crouched over the handlebars of a bike.

'Now what?' asks Guy.

'We grab him.'

'Don't be stupid!'

'There're two of us. We can get him into the VR equipment and that'll be that!' There is a chilling sense of finality to his words.

'At this time of night? Look, he would appear to be late getting home as it is. Another hour and you know what his mother will be doing – hitting the nines. The last thing you need, Darius, is the police snooping around your outfit looking for a missing boy.'

Darius stops the Range Rover. They watch the bike disappear out of sight into Smallham.

'I suppose you're right.'

'Of course I'm right. Don't go charging about, throwing your weight around. That was Harry's mistake last time. Pick him off, friendly like, just as you have all the others, with his dear mother's blessing.'

'How?'

'The opportunity will present itself, believe me,' says Guy. 'After all, we have the power.'

'You're right.' Darius smiles, a smile as icy as the late autumn rain teeming down the windscreen of the Range Rover. 'After all, we have the power.'

# 8

## 'Melvin! This is all your doing ...!'

'Mum! I can't come!'

'Of course you can!'

'I can't! I've got to see some people!'

'Too right you have, Melvin. And the people you've got to see are the assembled crowds at the Town Hall gallery.'

Melvin had forgotten about the Art Competition Prizegiving and Preview Evening. Seven thirty at the Town Hall. Precisely the time he was due to meet Cassandra and Bunny at the roundabout. Still, he knew how to get out of it.

He gambled on the fact that his mum or Hannah or Ellie would lose something. To tell the truth, it wasn't much of a gamble. His mum and sisters were always losing things.

This time it was the door keys.

'I'll stay and let you in, if you like ...'

'Melvin!'

By the time they eventually found them (in the freezer) it was already late. Melvin sauntered down the stairs. Time for him to reveal part two of his plan to get out of going to the Art Competition Prizegiving and Preview Evening.

'You're not wearing *that*!' screeched his mum, her eyes boggling.

'That' was part two of Melvin's plan. 'That' was Melvin's black *Lay of the Dork* tee-shirt.

'It's the only one I've got,' Melvin replied airily, 'All the others are in the wash.'

'All of them?'

'Yep.' Melvin had made well sure of that. He paused. 'Perhaps it would be better if you went without me . . . if you think I'm going to show you up.'

'You're coming with us.' Melvin's mum glowered. 'It's a proud and important moment for me and you're going to come and give me some support!'

'You're pathetic,' Hannah hissed in her brother's ear.

'Yeah,' agreed Ellie.

'Ellie, what are you doing?' sighed Mrs Perkins.

What Ellie was doing, it seemed to Melvin, was a kind of staccato, slow-motion dance, like one of those actors from black-and-white films.

'*Tobe!*' said Ellie.

'Tobe?'

'It's a dance. Jess taught me.'

'Did she now . . .' Melvin could tell his mum didn't approve of Jess.

'Yeah. They did it at Claire's birthday party.'

'And who's Claire?'

'Her sister. She's thirteen.'

Ellie made 'thirteen' sound like a magical number; an age when all the mysteries of the world (like what was the big deal about kissing boys) would be explained and all the injustices of the world (like not being allowed to read *Sweet Sixteen*) would be swept away. Melvin sighed. Sometimes he thought, it was as if Ellie came from another planet.

By the time they got to the Town Hall, they were running at least fifteen minutes late. A square-shouldered commissionaire hustled them into the gallery. Melvin blinked. The place was packed out. It seemed to him as if most of the women were wearing stuff made from curtains and most of the men were wearing bright red, green or mauve shoes; the sort of colours that Ellie had just grown out of.

'I want to go to the toilet,' announced Ellie, before they had hardly got in the door.

'I'll take her,' said Hannah.

Melvin and his mum sat down at the back. Melvin looked up towards the stage at the other end of the room. Behind a shining oak table stood Cassandra's mum, Councillor Mrs Washbone. On her left sat 'Gorgeous George', looking distinctly uncomfortable in a Paisley tie. On her right stood a towering suntanned figure with a smirk on his face as wide as a game show host's.

Darius O'Fee.

Melvin felt a great surge of panic rise in his

stomach. He must have gasped or something, because his mum turned to look at him with some concern. And that suddenly made it all right. He was with his mum. He was safe. Besides, the place was packed out with people. Darius O'Fee couldn't touch him in here.

Cassandra's mum was talking: '... All of us who are parents cannot but fail to have been impressed by the sterling work he has been doing with our young people at his Genius Academy. He has turned our rebellious youngsters into model citizens.'

There was a general murmuring of assent from the audience. Melvin felt sick, but he was wedged in tight.

'... So it is with especial pleasure that I call on Dr Darius O'Fee to announce the winner of the Smallham Amateur Art Competition.'

Darius O'Fee rose and smiled benignly down on the gathering. 'Thank you, Councillor Washbone, for those kind words of introduction. For my part, I've been thrilled by the talent and skills displayed by the young people of this town ...'

'Get on with it,' hissed Melvin's mum. She was fidgeting about, fiddling with her fingers, desperate to know who had won the Art Competition.

Darius O'Fee wasn't going to tell her. Yet.

'... And is this not a cause for joy? For our young people are our future. Our young people are the artists, the athletes, the leaders, the rulers of tomorrow.'

In a nightmarish flash, Melvin suddenly saw it all. Tomorrow's artists, athletes, leaders and rulers they might be; but as deadheads they would all be controlled by Darius O'Fee and whoever controlled his sinister organisation.

Melvin struggled to get up. He wanted to shout out, tell the stupid people that their children weren't being changed for the better; that the only thing they would become geniuses at was their ability to give unswerving obedience to Darius O'Fee. Whether anyone would have taken any notice of him if he had done, he was destined never to know, for his mum hauled him back down into his seat with a sharp tug.

'Sit down! He's announcing the winner!'

He was indeed. 'The winning picture,' drawled Darius O'Fee, 'is *Untitled* by Kate Perkins.'

A lot of things happened next.

A great cheer went up, led by Gorgeous George.

Darius O'Fee's piercing eyes swept back and forth across the room like searchlights, trying to pinpoint the winner.

Mrs Perkins gasped.

Melvin gulped.

For the winning work wasn't *Untitled* by Kate Perkins, but A-Lot-of-Yellow-Squiggles by Ellie Perkins. Melvin's brain went into overdrive. The reason for the mix-up was obvious. Copying Mum as usual, Ellie must have put her painting in the hall with the competition entries. That was why Gorgeous George had been expecting to pick up only five pictures, not six.

Gorgeous George had already pointed out Melvin's mum to Darius O'Fee. She was being beckoned forward to the platform.

'That's not mine!' she stuttered, in a surprisingly loud voice.

Cassandra's mum, Gorgeous George and Darius O'Fee stared at Melvin's mum. Then everyone turned round.

'Don't be shy, Kate! It's your name on the frame,' said Gorgeous George.

Melvin ducked down behind the woman in front of him, who was wearing a particularly large curtain. His face was alight.

'I know, but . . .' Melvin's mum's brain had also been in overdrive and she had no doubt as to whose fault this embarrassing disaster was. 'Melvin! This is all your doing!' she thundered.

An astonished gasp ran round the room. Melvin was desperate to become invisible. Suddenly the gasp became a cheer and everyone began clapping and whistling wildly. Melvin found himself grabbed by the shoulder and propelled forward, bouncing off the assembled arty-types like a ball on a pinball machine, towards the platform.

'No!' he tried to say, but it wouldn't come out.

Councillor Washbone pumped his hand like she was trying to pull a pint of beer.

'Well done, Melvin! Your mother must be proud of you! It really is a quite . . . er *amazing* picture!'

Next it was the turn of Melvin's art teacher to congratulate him on his stunning painting.

'You're a dark horse, Melvin!'

Then Melvin found himself looking up into the menacing stare of Darius O'Fee.

'Quite an achievement,' hissed Darius O'Fee in his ear. Melvin caught the edge of sarcasm in his voice. Suddenly, he grasped Melvin's arm tightly and raised his other arm for silence. His command was obeyed.

'This young man's native talent as artist shines forth as an example to us all,' he declared. 'Here is someone whose potential genius is here for us all to behold.'

Everyone's eyes were fixed on Ellie's squiggles.

'I shall take this young man,' continued Darius O'Fee, 'and I shall nurture his genius. In a few years, just as the name Constable is synonymous with Suffolk, just as the name Renoir is synonymous with Paris, so the name Perkins shall be synonymous with Smallham.'

A huge cheer went up. Flash bulbs popped. You would have thought that being next to the museum and library, people would have conducted their conversations in discreet whispers. But no, there was shouting, calling out, yelling and laughing. There was pushing and shoving as everyone surged forward to get a better look at UNTITLED. The thought crossed Melvin's troubled mind that if 8GG had been caught behaving in such a fashion during art, Bomber Buzzard would have bunged them all on report for a month.

'Melvin? Melvin? A bit stunned, are you?'

A tall young woman with a notebook was shouting at Melvin:

'Janey Winkle – I'm from the *Gazette*, Melvin. How old are you?'

Before Melvin could answer, a hand grabbed his shoulder from behind. A fresh-faced youth shouted in his ear:

'Town Council public relations. Do you spell Melvin with a "y" or an "i"?'

'With an "i",' murmured Darius O'Fee. He held Melvin firmly by the elbow and steered him off the stage into the body of the hall. People stood back, beaming at them.

Melvin's mum flung her arms around him. Her anger and disappointment had given way to excitement and pride. 'You silly boy! Why didn't you say you were into art?'

'But, Mum, I'm – '

'If you like, Mrs Perkins, Melvin could join our special residential weekend. It's already under way.'

95

'Oh, I think he'd like that, wouldn't you, Melvin?'

'No, Mum!'

'I expect the excitement's got to him a bit,' Mrs Perkins whispered to Darius O'Fee.

The Director of the Genius Academy smiled understandingly.

'No, Mum!'

'Melvin, if you're thinking of the money . . . well, you've got your prize money now!'

'Oh, I think we can forget the fee,' Darius O'Fee waved his arms about expansively. 'He'll need that for the future. Materials aren't cheap.'

'No, Dr O'Fee, we couldn't possibly . . .'

'No, we couldn't!' agreed Melvin.

'I insist!' insisted Darius O'Fee. 'I can spot true artistic talent when I see it.'

Melvin's mum flushed with pride. 'To think, we've got a real artist in the family!'

'He gets it from you, Kate.' Gorgeous George had sidled up and was standing close – very close – to Melvin's mum. She smiled, sheepishly.

'Perhaps we will all have that painting holiday in a gypsy caravan after all!' She almost seemed to be including Gorgeous George in the 'we'.

'Mum! You don't understand, I didn't do – '

'I'll bring your pyjamas and toothbrush up to the Genius Academy later . . .'

'Mum. I don't want to go!'

'If he's unhappy, you can always take him home

96

when you come,' said Darius O'Fee, his voice oozing with concern and consideration. 'But I'm sure, once he sees our art and craft studio facilities, you won't be able to drag him away!'

Before Melvin had a chance to say or do anything further, there was a whooshing sound behind him, then an almost imperceptible shove from Darius O'Fee, who was still gripping his elbow, and Melvin found himself in the lift.

Out of the corner of his eye, he saw Hannah and Ellie looking at UNTITLED. He heard Ellie telling Councillor Washbone, 'I did that!' Councillor Washbone was smiling at her condescendingly.

Then the lift doors thudded shut.

Darius O'Fee did not let go of Melvin's elbow.

Not until they were safely in the Range Rover. Melvin looked at the door handle. Darius O'Fee caught his look.

'The doors are locked,' he smirked.

Melvin's hand moved down the side of his seat.

'And so is your seat belt.'

# IX

Already the cold night rain has turned the golden autumn leaves a murky brown. The white Range Rover speeds through Smallham High Street and bears sharp right up Hogman's Hill towards the darkness of the South Downs.

The driver is singing. 'Lucky, lucky, lucky...!'

He turns to his young passenger. 'I was getting just a little worried, Melvin.'

His young passenger says nothing.

'I was beginning to wonder just how I could persuade you back to the Genius Academy, and here you are, delivered up unto me in the most unexpected way!' The driver bends close to his passenger's face. 'After all, you are – how shall I put it? – the missing link. The only member of your class not a fully participating member of the Academy.'

Still his young passenger says nothing. The Range Rover sweeps into the drive of Hogman's Thorn House, its powerful headlamps lighting up the solid wrought iron gates.

'Here we are,' says the driver. 'Journey's end.'

# 9

## 'Melvin! Melvin! Here we come ... !'

Melvin's brain hadn't been idle during the drive. If he could keep Darius O'Fee from marching him off to the deadheading room until his mum came with his pyjamas, he could still escape. Perhaps he wouldn't need to. Perhaps Bunny and Cas had worked out what it was that had un-deadheaded her. Perhaps even now they were up at Hogman's Thorn House putting a plan into action.

As they drew up outside the massive front door, four figures appeared in the porch. Darius' window slid down and spatters of cold rain blew into the Range Rover. Melvin saw that the four figures were all of College student age and all wearing grey sweatshirts with SMALLHAM YOUTH ARTS & SPORTS ACADEMY emblazoned across them in bright red letters.

They all smiled; brightly, inanely. Their dull eyes said it all: deadheads. So his classmates weren't the first, thought Melvin. There were others who had been deadheaded. He wondered how many and where they came from.

'Everything okay?' called out Darius.

'Yes, fine!' called back one of the four.

Perhaps if I can keep them talking like this, Mum will soon be here with my pyjamas.

'Good. Melvin here is raring for a go on our Virtual Reality game.'

Darius got out. Then he went round the side to let Melvin out. The four deadheads surrounded the door. There was no way Melvin could make a run for it.

'I'll just park the jeep,' said Darius.

The four deadheads guided Melvin inside. Everything was as calm and as orderly as it had been when Melvin had last fled the place. No Cassandra; no Bunny.

'Hi, Melvin!' Pravi was heading for the coffee bar. He wore a grey sweatshirt. Everyone was wearing a grey sweatshirt. Everyone except Melvin.

'Darius will be with you shortly,' said one of the deadheads who had escorted him in. Melvin heard the key turn in the lock. Then two of them disappeared into Darius' office, while the other two headed for the coffee bar.

Hide! was Melvin's first thought.

Escape! was his second.

The fire escape! was his third.

He remembered that during the WhoppaShoppa business, he had seen a fire escape leading down from an attic light. An attic that had obviously been servants' quarters once upon a time. In which case, the way up there would be via some back stairs.

Melvin sauntered to the foot of the main staircase.

'Hi, Melvin!' smiled Jodie Jenkins.

'Hi!' said Melvin.

'Would you like to listen to some Cliff Richard CDs with me?'

'Er... I'm a bit busy right at this moment,' said Melvin.

Out of the coffee bar came one of the deadheads who had brought him in. Instinctively, without thinking, Melvin quickened his pace up the stairs.

'Melvin!' The deadhead's tone was firm, cold and frightening.

Melvin ran.

The deadhead took a whistle from her pocket and blew long and hard.

Melvin was already at the top of the staircase. Below him, his classmates appeared in every doorway.

'Fetch Melvin!' intoned the deadhead. Nobody moved. Then the deadhead added, 'It is what Darius wishes.'

Immediately, Pravi, Sarah, Jodie and the rest of 8GG bounded up the staircase in pursuit of Melvin.

'Melvin! Melvin! Here we come!' they chanted.

Melvin knew he had no way to go but up. It would lead to the fire escape; besides any other downstairs exit was blocked now. He raced along the first floor corridor. There were doors on either side. Bedrooms or dormitories, they had to be.

'Melvin! Melvin! Here we come!' The chanting was getting closer.

At the end of the corridor, Melvin saw another door, slightly smaller than the others. He prayed it would not be locked.

'Melvin! Melvin! Here we come!' the voices cried, only a couple of metres behind him now.

As Melvin grabbed the doorhandle, he just caught the faint sound of another fainter voice behind him: 'No, Perkins!'

The door opened easily. Too easily. In the doorway stood Darius O'Fee. He raised his hand in a kind of half instruction, half salute. The running feet stood still. The chanting stopped.

'Victoria, Gil, I may need your help. The rest of you may return to your activities,' said Darius O'Fee. As one, the deadheads turned and walked back down the corridor; except two of the quartet who had escorted Melvin from the Range Rover to the house.

'So, you managed to find your own way to the games room, Melvin? I'm impressed by your enthusiasm.'

Darius shut the door. Melvin found himself looking at a large metal-framed, black-seated, swivel chair. It reminded him of something, something he couldn't quite place ... a dentist's chair? No ... Above it was a large glass dome. On the armrests, a pair of black gauntlets. On the footrest, a pair of what looked like giant's feet warmers. All just as Cassandra had described.

Melvin struggled, of course. But there were three of them and only one of him.

As soon as his arms were strapped to the sides of the chair, he knew what it reminded him of. It wasn't a dentist's chair. It was an executioner's electric chair.

'Relax, Melvin. You want to become a great artist. It is what your mother wishes.'

Melvin's head began to fill with sensations. He could see, hear, touch, taste and smell . . . It was glorious . . .


Mrs Perkins was surprised to find the main door locked. A very pleasant young man in a grey sweatshirt opened it.

'We have to keep it locked. For security reasons. We're a bit isolated up here.'

'Of course.' Mrs Perkins thought it a most wise precaution.

She didn't have to wait long in the bright and cosy office before Darius O'Fee appeared with Melvin.

'I've packed an extra pair of socks.'

Melvin smiled.

'You're quite sure you want to stay?'

'Oh yes,' said Melvin. 'I intend to work hard at my painting.'

'Good,' said Mrs Perkins. She felt uneasy, but she couldn't work out why. 'I'll see you on Sunday evening then . . .'

'Yes,' said Melvin.

'I said you wouldn't be able to drag him away, didn't I!' laughed Darius O'Fee.

Mrs Perkins shivered slightly. She wrapped her arms about herself, as if she was feeling cold. Darius saw it, but said nothing. Mrs Perkins smiled weakly and left. Darius went through to the office. Melvin wandered along the hall towards the coffee bar.

'Hi, Melvin!'

'Hi, Pravi.'

'Fancy a few rounds of Arm Wrestling?'

'No, thanks . . . I've got to be careful of my hands.'

'Oh?'

'Yes. I'm going to become a world famous artist.'

'Are you?'

'Oh yes.' Melvin smiled blankly. 'It's what my mother wishes.'

# X

*In the farmhouse kitchen the phone rings. The woman answers it.*

*'Hello?'*

*'Angie? It's Darius. You can tell Guy he was right. The opportunity did present itself. It might have been the power, it might've been luck. Whatever, the boy has been delivered into my hands. It was a bit of a struggle but he played the game in the end. Any danger he may have presented, is now past.'*

*'And there are no other problems?'*

*'No! None at all. Why should there be?'*

*He didn't mention the strange sensations of chill that suddenly seemed to close in on him for no apparent reason. It was simply a draughty old house, he told himself.*

# 10

## 'The witching hour . . .'

The boys in the dormitory at Hogman's Thorn House were all sleeping. One or two pulled their duvets up closer under their chins as if the night air had suddenly got colder.

'Perkins! Wake up!'

If he'd had the ability, the ghost of Arnold Thomas would surely have hauled Melvin out of his bed and shaken him into consciousness with his bare hands.

'Perkins, old friend, what have they done to you?'

Melvin stirred, looked up. If he did see the young ghost, he did not acknowledge him. Instead he slipped off his bed and wandered in an aimless sort of way out of the half-lit dormitory, along a corridor and into a large, curtainless room that housed the boys' showers and toilets. The ghost of Arnold Thomas glided along behind him agitatedly.

Melvin turned and faced the ghost. 'Evening, Arnold,' he said.

'Oh, Perkins, thank goodness. I thought they'd got you,' said Arnold.

'They very nearly did,' said Melvin. 'And if it hadn't been for you, they would have done.'

'My presence helped then?'

'Your presence saved me.'

'I'd seen what that confounded contraption did to your friends. That's why I interposed myself when I did.'

Melvin shuddered at the thought of just how close he had been to becoming a deadhead. The VR helmet, the gauntlets, the boots had all been on. He had felt himself drifting off into another world, another reality, a reality that had been slowly enveloping him, like a luscious, wonderful, careless dream.

Then he had heard Arnold's voice.

'Perkins, you imbecile! Did I not warn you? Did I not tell you of the dangers of this place? You will become as the rest of them and then I'll have nobody, but nobody to help me avenge my murder. Come back here, Perkins, do you hear me?'

Melvin had heard him all right – and seen him, the ghost of Arnold Thomas, dancing before the deadheading dream, in effect shielding his eyes from the images in the Virtual Reality game. Melvin had known then, that providing Arnold stayed around fluttering in front of the visions, shouting above the sounds, deadheading would not work on him.

When Darius O'Fee had eventually led him out of the swivel chair, Melvin still had not the faintest desire to become an artist.

'What is your ambition, Melvin?' Darius O'Fee had asked.

Melvin had known the answer: 'To become an artist,' he had said. 'It is what my mother wishes of me.'

Keeping up the pretence at being a deadhead had been easier than he had expected, except when his mum had arrived.

'Take me home!' he had wanted to say.

But he had known he couldn't. He had a job to do: to put an end to Darius O'Fee's terrifying experiment and to save his friends. He wondered how long he could keep up the pretence, now that every moment had become a moment of fear. Fear that somebody, Darius O'Fee or one of the other deadheads, would notice, suspect something. Fear that time was running out for his friends.

'I've got to stop him,' Melvin said to Arnold.

'Them,' corrected Arnold.

'Them. What are they, Arnold? A secret organisation of some sort?'

Arnold shrugged. 'Of two things I am certain: they have some sort of especial bond and they all have some connection with this House. That is the only explanation for their need to work from here. They are aware of its power and are using... or rather abusing it.'

Melvin yawned. He felt suddenly tired.

'You need some sleep, Perkins.'

'It's dangerous to sleep with all this going on. Supposing Darius O'Fee tried something . . .'

'Why should he? He believes he has done all he needs to do with you. I shall wake you, if there is any sign of danger.'

'You won't go to sleep?'

'Ghosts don't sleep. Would that we could. At least then we could dream. You are safe enough, Perkins. Remember you have the power of the House to draw on, too.'

'And what will that enable me to do? Wrestle Darius O'Fee to the ground with my bare hands?'

'Who knows?' said Arnold.

The fluorescent light above them flickered on and off nervously. Arnold seemed to be dancing in and out of the light.

Melvin looked at him. Suddenly something clicked in his brain. 'Oh my goodness,' he whispered. 'I know what it was.'

'Know what what was?'

'What turned Cassandra. I know how to reverse the deadheading process. I know how to bring Pravi, Sarah and the rest of them back!'

'As I said, this House has strange powers, Perkins.'

Every time Melvin thought he must be asleep, he found himself awake wondering what time Cassandra would arrive in the morning. Wondering how he would let her know he was not a deadhead. Wondering how he could possibly find a way to tell her about his discovery.

Even so, when the surprisingly bright October sunlight burst through the long dormitory windows, he was snoring loudly. Then something woke him with a start. A sound – a sound of someone in the distance, screaming. Melvin sat up and listened. No, it wasn't screaming; it was too controlled, too lacking in fear for that. He looked around him. Pravi slept on in the bed next to his, bedside cabinet stacked high with maths textbooks. In the corner, Damien Higgins was getting dressed, seemingly oblivious to the tortured cries that echoed from room to room.

Melvin listened again. Now the sound seemed strangely familiar. He had heard it before ... at where ...? At school. In Expressive Arts. The picture in his mind came to him in a flash. Cas Washbone, singing, as only Cas could sing: loudly, raucously, off key.

He got up and went down to breakfast. Arnold slid silently along, a few paces behind him. Breakfast was creepy. The deadheads munched their toast and cornflakes, quietly, purposely. There was no giggling, no fooling around, no chatter. It was like having breakfast in a crowded dentist's waiting room. All the faces were dull, as if they were somewhere else. He saw Cassandra, sharing a corner

110

table with Jodie and Kayleigh.

Then without warning, everybody got to their feet. He had no idea how it started, but it made him shake from head to foot.

'Darius!' The voices in the hall cried out as one. 'Darius! Darius! Darius!'

Darius O'Fee marched in. He stood at the front of the hall, twisting his face into what Melvin presumed he thought was a captivating smile. The chanting got louder. Melvin joined in, knowing that not to would arouse suspicion, until Darius O'Fee slowly raised his arm. Then it stopped.

'My young friends,' said Darius O'Fee; his voice calm, soothing, barely raised above a whisper. 'This morning we must bid welcome to a new member to our select band. Melvin Perkins!'

With a start, Melvin realised that everyone had turned round to look at him. Then they broke out into applause. Melvin stood in his place, praying that doing nothing, saying nothing was the right thing.

Everybody in the hall formed themselves into a line. They did this silently, expertly, as if they all knew where they should be. Pravi, Sarah, Jodie, Kayleigh and all the rest of the Norman Burke pupils then greeted him:

'Hi, Melvin! Welcome, Melvin!'

Then each of them shook hands with him. Every hand Melvin shook was as smooth and as

111

cold as stone.

Cassandra was the last.

'Hi, Melvin! Welcome, Melvin!'

Melvin took her hand. And found it was warm. He wanted to jump for joy. He wanted to hug Cassandra. Instead he kept his face impassive. Instead, he felt his hand being squeezed. He squeezed back; just so Cassandra would know that he hadn't been deadheaded.

'Come, Melvin!' called Darius O'Fee. 'I shall direct you to the art studio. We shall make a start on your future as an artist of great genius.'

'It is what my mother wishes,' said Melvin.

Melvin spent the morning in the art studio painting red and blue splodges on pieces of paper. He spent the afternoon in the art studio painting yellow and mauve splodges on pieces of paper. All the time he was thinking: when – and how – would he get the opportunity to tell Cassandra that he knew how she had been turned back from being a deadhead? The problem was, he was never alone. There was always one of the twentysomething deadheads lurking silently in another part of the room. Once or twice Arnold drifted by, cast a puzzled look at Melvin's canvas then drifted on.

It was just before tea when Cassandra appeared in the studio.

'Hi, Melvin!'

'Hi, Cassandra!'

Victoria, the twentysomething deadhead lurking about the back of the studio, looked up. She appeared to be paying no attention, but Melvin guessed that she was all ears.

'That is a fine painting,' said Cassandra.

'Thank you.'

'It's so . . . deep . . . so full of meaning.'

'Is it?'

'Yes!' Cassandra was insistent. 'That sweeping branch of an oak tree . . .'

Melvin stared at the yellow and mauve squiggles in front of him.

'. . . And the two figures underneath . . . with that old clock between them.'

Melvin stared some more at the yellow and mauve squiggles in front of him. And then suddenly, he understood just what Cassandra was really saying.

'Ah yes . . .' he said. 'I see what you mean. With its hands pointing to midnight.'

'Midnight . . .' echoed Cassandra.

'The witching hour,' said Melvin. And then wished he hadn't.

Cassandra met his eyes. Melvin realised this was his chance to tell her what he knew.

'This is my technique,' said Melvin.

He took a blank sheet of paper and painted six large letters on it.

# STROBE

'Hmmm . . .' Cassandra frowned, for all the world as if she was trying to understand a bizarre artistic theory of some sort. Then: 'Crikey Mikey!' she hissed.

And Melvin knew she understood.

The twentysomething deadhead looked up.

'. . . Crikey Mikey, it *is* good, Melvin. Very clever. How you manage it I don't know,' said Cassandra quickly, desperately covering her tracks. 'Now I simply must go and practise my scales. And you, of course, must paint.'

She turned and left. Melvin took his brush, thrust it into the pot. Then all over the six letters which had meant so much to Cassandra he painted a bold mauve tree, two matchstick men and a clock face showing twelve o'clock.

Just in case the deadhead at the back of the room decided to wander over and take a look.

Arnold shouted in his ear at five to twelve, but he was already awake.

He made his way along the richly carpeted corridors, then down the main staircase. He reached up to slide open the bolt on the front door and found it had already been pulled. Cassandra must be waiting for him, he thought.

'I suppose you would like me to haunt the staff

quarters and to warn you of any danger.'

'What else are ghosts for?' hissed Melvin, as Arnold drifted off back up the staircase.

The night was sharp and bright. He made his way along the side of the house and began to follow the wall towards the branch of the oak tree they had used to get into the grounds back in the summer. The wall was now topped all the way round with barbed wire.

She was huddled right against the wall under the branch. She was wearing a pale blue towelling dressing gown. This and the way the moonlight gave her face a cool pallor made her seem strangely unfamiliar to Melvin. But the way she pushed her dark hair back from her face before she spoke was recognisable enough.

'Bet you never thought art could be that useful.'

Melvin shrugged. Neither of them said anything for a moment. Then Cassandra spoke.

'Tell me then! What on earth dragged you up here and how come you didn't get deadheaded?'

Melvin explained about the Art Competition and how he had been brought up to Hogman's Thorn House by Darius O'Fee.

'And he put you through the Virtual Reality game?'

Melvin nodded.

'Why didn't it work?'

'Something . . . somebody helped me . . .'

Cassandra looked him full in the face. Her dark eyes narrowed.

'Your ghost friend? That Pravi Patel's always laughing about?'

She wasn't laughing, Melvin noticed. He nodded.

'You're something else, Melvin Perkins, you really are.'

Melvin wasn't quite sure what she meant, and he doubted whether she quite knew herself.

'So how did you work out that I'd been un-dead-headed by a strobe light?'

'I was in the toilets . . .'

'Fascinating . . .'

'And the fluorescent bulb was flickering and – ' Melvin didn't want to mention Arnold again, so he said, 'and it made me blink and everything looked jerky. It reminded me of my little sister. She'd been doing a really weird dance she called her *tobe* dance. She'd got it from her friend Jess, who'd learnt it at her big sister's birthday party. Her big sister Claire.'

'The same party I was at!'

'Yes. Ellie can't say "s" properly.'

'Tobe dancing is strobe dancing.'

'Yep. It all fell into place. The Virtual Reality game deadheads people by giving the brain powerful false messages about what is real and what isn't real. Strobes do the same thing. The way you see people dancing under a strobe isn't the way they're really dancing.'

116

'And they can be quite dangerous, you know. They can do your brain in.'

'Yeah, I'd heard that.' Melvin suddenly kicked at the turf, angrily. 'It doesn't help us very much, does it?'

'Why not?'

'Where are we going to get a strobe light from?'

'On the lighting gantry in the drama studio.'

'Eh?'

'Bunny brought it up here just after tea.'

'How?'

'In the van.'

'I meant how – without Darius or his helpers seeing him?'

'Oh, they all saw him. Darius even gave him a hand to get it rigged. . . . He thinks it's a special piece of equipment for my performance to the parents tomorrow evening, which it is really, I suppose.'

'But how did Bunny know . . . about the strobe?'

Cas thrust her hand into her dressing-gown pocket.

'I told him!'

She waved a tiny mobile phone at Melvin. 'You don't think I'd come up here for the weekend without this, do you?'

They walked back to the house in the darkness.

'I've worked out a plan. Simple really,' said Cas. 'At the parents' do tomorrow, when I come on to

117

sing my two arias . . .'

Melvin shuddered at the thought.

'. . . Gil – or whichever deadhead is on the lighting board – will switch the strobe on, thinking it's just another spotlight. Every deadhead in the hall will be brought back to reality. Great, isn't it! We get creepy Gil and the rest of them to do all the work for us. So simple!'

Too simple, thought Melvin. But he didn't say so. He had no better ideas.

They reached the door. Melvin saw that Cas was staring at him.

'What *is* that?'

'What?'

'On your dressing-gown pocket?'

'Oh. Superman.'

'Superman?'

'I can't help it. I've had this dressing gown since I was nine,' explained Melvin crossly. 'Mum says she won't buy me another one until I've grown another two sizes at least.'

Cas shook her head. 'Parents!'

Melvin nodded.

'You go in first,' whispered Cas. 'You know, just in case . . .'

'Just in case what?'

'Just in case anyone's about. It wouldn't do for both of us to be caught, would it?'

'No,' agreed Melvin, thinking that it wouldn't do

for *either* of them to be caught.

Cas was standing quite close to him. He could see her breath drifting off into the night air. He caught her dark eyes before she looked quickly away. Suddenly, he felt her squeeze his hand.

'Just making sure. That you're not a deadhead,' she whispered.

# XI

Darius O'Fee's bedroom, of course, is on the dark side of the house. Still half asleep, he pulls the covers closer. Despite the October night being unseasonably warm, he feels there is a chill to the room. It is this which wakes him.

Once awake he is restless.

He steps out of his bedroom and into the corridor.

Halfway down the staircase he sees the boy.

'Melvin?'

Melvin does not reply.

Darius O'Fee follows him, all the way back to the boys' dormitory. There Melvin Perkins slips off his shoes and dressing gown and climbs into bed.

Sleepwalking? He has to be. The boy has been thoroughly deadheaded. He can pose no danger to the experiment now.

Darius O'Fee is about to turn when he notices Melvin's arm. Beneath his pyjama cuff there protrudes a jumper cuff. Beneath the jumper cuff there protrudes a shirt cuff. Darius O'Fee is not a stupid man.

He creeps silently up to Melvin's bedside.

'Come with me, Melvin,' he whispers.

## 11

## 'Activate Plan B . . .!'

'Come with me, Melvin.'

Melvin opened his eyes and stared straight into the shadowy face of Darius O'Fee.

'Sleepwalkers don't get fully dressed before they go walking in their sleep, Melvin.'

Arnold had warned him, of course, that Darius was on his way, but not soon enough. 'Say nothing. Pretend you're sleepwalking!' had been Arnold's suggestion.

Melvin climbed out of bed.

'Time to play the Virtual Reality game, Melvin. But this time, I think you should play for a very long time indeed.'

How long? thought Melvin. Too long for Arnold's intervention to work again? All of a sudden he panicked. He couldn't face the gauntlets and the boots; couldn't face the thought of the glass dome descending over his head.

So he ran for it.

His fleetness of foot took Darius by surprise. It took Melvin by surprise. Was it just fear, or was there somewhere deep inside him some sort of power which he was drawing from the House?

Darius took a whistle from his pocket and blew long and hard. Pravi, Damien and the rest of the boys in the dormitory had already been woken by the sound of voices. As one they stepped from their beds and ran after Melvin.

'Melvin! Melvin! Here we come!'

Back along the corridor Melvin ran, his only thought: to get out of the house, out of the grounds, away from Darius O'Fee, away from the deadheads.

He reached the top of the stairs. Already the girls were coming at him from the opposite corridor, led by twentysomething deadhead, Victoria.

'Melvin! Melvin! Here we come!'

Melvin leapt off the stairs, then stopped as he saw Cas. She held her mobile to her mouth.

'Activate Plan B!' she yelled, then turned to Melvin. 'You won't get any further than the gates! The drama studio! It's our only chance!'

Melvin ran after her into the studio. The deadheads were closing in on him. They formed a circle round him, their faces blank with menace.

'Melvin! Melvin! Here we come!'

In came Darius.

Then out went the lights.

And on came the strobe.

Shafts of piercing white light shot through the darkened room. In the shafts, pale figures jerked and jolted about, struggling to shield their eyes, stumbling to get out of the light. The sight was terrifying, but it was strangely quiet: deadheads aren't programmed to speak out of turn.

Melvin could just see the figure of Darius O'Fee making his way across the floor. He seemed to be going ever so slowly, but that Melvin guessed was because of the strobe light. There was no doubt who he was making for, though: Cas. She saw him, too, and already began to make her way to the door, Darius in her wake. Like two mad puppets, they shimmered and stabbed their way across the room.

Out into the hall and up the stairs went Cas, Darius close on her heels.

'After them, Perkins!' cried an animated voice beside him.

Thank you, Arnold.

After them Melvin went.

Where is she going? thought Melvin.

Along the top corridor, past the dormitories was where she was heading. In the direction of a small door.

'No, Cas!'

But Cas was already through it and into the Virtual Reality room.

Melvin stopped for just a second. Perkins' First Law of Survival (Keep Your Head Down) flashed across his mind. He thought of going back. It wasn't a thought that lasted for long. He charged in. Cas was hitting out at the VR equipment, trying to smash it up. Darius O'Fee was trying to grab hold of her. Cas lashed out at the gauntlets, the chair, the stack of electronic black metal boxes carrying the game's brains. All she did was to bruise her hand. Already Darius was pulling her into the chair.

'Stand back,' he screamed breathlessly at Melvin. 'Or I'll smash your head against the wall.'

Melvin dived to the floor and grabbed a handful of cables that he saw leading from the control boxes. He pulled them, hard. The boxes wobbled. He pulled them even harder, with a strength he didn't realise he had. The stack slowly toppled. There were a few sparks, a bang and a little smoke. That was all. Like a dud firework.

Cas was kicking out at Darius, who had turned his attention to Melvin. Melvin fought him off, desperately, hysterically; no experienced fighter was he. Darius grabbed Melvin's neck, his head, to beat it on the floor. Melvin tried to get him with his knees, then his feet, but the air was going from his lungs.

Suddenly, the grip around his neck slackened. Melvin could hear a familiar noise. And so could Darius.

Sirens.

'You little fools!' hissed Darius.

Already he was off Melvin and had his hand on the door.

'Don't you know who holds the real power in all this?'

He opened the door and was gone.

'Come on!' yelled Cas, hauling a dazed, exhausted and bruised Melvin to his feet. 'It's Plan B!'

'Is it?'

'Yeah! I rang Bunny! Every emergency vehicle in Smallham will be up here soon.'

Melvin stumbled to his feet and followed Cas out of the VR room and back along the corridor. Just as they passed the boys' dormitory, a dark figure charged out, waving a hatchet.

It was a firefighter.

The drama studio was utter chaos.

Cas and Melvin's schoolmates were mooching around with the dazed look of people who have just had blindfolds removed.

Firefighters sauntered about looking for smoke.

Two paramedics scanned the room for signs of blood.

A policeman in a flak jacket was trying to establish who was in charge.

'Dr O'Fee . . .' someone said.

But of Dr O'Fee and his four helper deadheads there was no sign. The white Range Rover was no longer in the garage, either.

'What's been going on here, then?' asked the policeman.

No one could rightly say.

'Looks like a fire drill,' said a firefighter.

'If there's no one in charge of you kids, you'll all

have to go home.'

A quarter of an hour later, the parents began to arrive. Kayleigh's dad was first, bleary-eyed, unshaven.

'Where is he?' he demanded. 'I'll give him Genius Academy, smarmy little toe-rag.'

'We'll do our best to find Dr O'Fee,' said the police officer, 'but as far as we can ascertain, he has committed no crime.'

'I'll commit a crime on him,' said Jodie's mum, who had appeared completely unrecognised by anyone, because she'd never been out in public without make-up before.

'Where are all your Cliff Richard CDs, Jodie?'

'Stuff Cliff Richard,' said Jodie.

Slowly, one by one, Cas and Melvin's schoolmates departed.

'Do you want a lift with me?' Pravi asked Melvin.

'Nah, thanks, Pravi, but Cas's brother's taking me.'

Pravi raised an eyebrow. 'May the trusty stave of the Brummis protect you!'

Yes, Pravi was back to normal.

'It worked, Cas.'

'Seems to have. No more singing!'

'No more painting!'

'Everyone back to normal.'

'Except Damien. I heard him telling his mum he wants to carry on with ballroom dancing lessons.'

'Given his lack of skills as a footballer, that's probably no bad thing,' reckoned Cas.

The streets of Smallham were deserted as Bunny's old van rattled and spluttered its way towards Melvin's house.

'No more Genius Academy.'

'No more deadheads.'

'I didn't say that,' murmured Melvin.

'Next time, we'll be more than ready for them,' said Bunny. 'Two nil! Two nil!' he sang. It was meant to sound funny, but neither Cas nor Melvin laughed.

'Melvin and me were almost killed tonight, you wally!' Cas shouted angrily at her brother.

'Sorry.'

Bunny brought the van to a halt outside Melvin's house and turned off the engine. Cas got out to let Melvin down. She followed him up his front path.

'What are you doing?'

'Walking with you up your front path. I've already let you out of my sight once tonight and look what happened.'

Melvin managed a grin.

'Aren't you going to thank me for saving your life?'

'Thanks,' said Melvin.

Cassandra stood there. 'And . . .?'

'And what?'

127

'You looked as if you were going to say something else.'

'No . . .'

'You were!'

Melvin swallowed. 'Thanks for not laughing about Arnold.'

'Your ghost?'

Melvin nodded.

Cas spoke quietly: 'You will tell me about him sometime, won't you?'

Melvin felt his hand being squeezed. This time, he knew, she wasn't just making sure he wasn't a deadhead. He squeezed back and was surprised at how small her hand felt in his. As he turned his head away, he felt the slightest of kisses brush his cheek.

''Night, Superman,' said Cas.

When he looked up, Cas was already running back to the van. She climbed in, waved, then brushed her dark hair back from her face.

Melvin sat on the doorstep and watched as cloud after cloud scudded across the bright October sky. So many questions drifted through his head. How could he avenge Arnold's murder? Why had *he* and no one else been empowered to see Arnold? Who were the people trying to deadhead the population of Smallham? Why did his mum go weak at the knees over an ageing hippy called George? Why had his dad left home? So many questions.

128

As his key turned silently in the front door, he felt an overwhelming need to be in possession of the answers.

He determined there and then that he was going to find them.

And, although this idea was half hidden by all the others, he had the crazy idea that Cas Washbone would be helping him.

# XII

There are four of them. Three men and a woman. They sit around the gnarled table in the farmhouse kitchen, stony-faced.

'Dear me, you are quiet, Darius,' sneers Harry.

'That VR equipment . . . it was state of the art . . . the latest from the States . . . CIA approved . . . the lot.' Darius addresses no one in particular.

'Too state of the art, if you ask me,' snarls Guy. 'The more sophisticated a piece of technology is, the easier it is to foul it up. Look what happened when corporations first started installing computer networks. They could be hacked into by any spotty adolescent with a GCSE in Computer Studies.'

'But the boy knows something. I'm sure of it.' Darius' voice has an almost pleading tone.

'How could he? Unless someone has blabbed?'

'No one blabbed,' says Darius.

'I know Melvin Perkins. He's not exactly Sherlock Holmes,' says Guy sarcastically.

'I think it's to do with the House.'

'Darius, your mind's going. We're the only ones who are empowered. You know that.'

Angela speaks. Her tone is clipped, efficient. 'The

*point is, if we don't get the experiment up and running and deadhead Smallham in the next nine months, our customers aren't going to buy.'*

*'You've got a plan?' inquires Guy.*

*'I have. And believe me, it will work. We have governments and corporations the world over waiting on our deadheading experiment. A couple of stroppy schoolkids aren't going to be allowed to get in the way. Do you understand?'*

*The others understand. For there is a ruthlessness in her voice which silences any doubts or objections that they might be harbouring.*

# 1

## *The Haunting*

Melvin Perkins' First Law of Survival is: Keep Your Head Down. Unfortunately, fate's First Law of Survival is: Get Perkins.

Only Melvin knows the cause of the terrifying condition that has afflicted his mum and all the other adults in town. Their eyes have become dull and unseeing and their minds lifeless. They have, in effect, been turned into Deadheads. How can Melvin bring his mum and the rest of the Deadheads back to life, particularly as his only helpmate is the ghost of a Victorian juvenile delinquent?

# 2

## *The Genius Academy*

When Cassandra Washbone, the tone-deaf school troublemaker, announces that she's going to become an opera singer, Melvin is appalled. Such an awful idea can mean only one thing: the Deadheads are back. Fate intervenes when Melvin accidentally wins the local children's art competition and finds himself at the mercy of the sinister wonder-worker, Darius O'Fee.

What is the secret behind the mysterious Genius Academy? Melvin must find out before he, Cassandra and all of their friends are turned into Deadheads...

This is the second in a series of four gripping thrillers chronicling Melvin Perkins' battle against the Deadheads.

# 3

## *The Vanishing Faces*

When New Age travellers camp in the grounds of Hogman's Thorn House, local TV news reporter Angie Allbright befriends them. Then Melvin realises her face is dreadfully familiar – and not just because it is on the TV screens every day. So when Gem, a young traveller girl, goes missing, his worst fears are confirmed: the Deadheads have returned.

How can Melvin and his unlikely ally Cas Washbone stop Angie Allbright from carrying out the most daring and chilling deadeading experiment of all?

***Available Spring 1998***

**Melvin**

**and the DEADHEADS**

# 4

### *The Avenger*

For Melvin and Cas, the time of final reckoning arrives when they are lured straight to the Deadheads' headquarters. The sinister gang is desperate – intelligence services and criminal organisations the world over are demanding to see results.

But Melvin now knows the truth: about the power of Hogman's Thorn House and the Deadheads; about Arnold the Victorian ghost; about his own past – and about himself. Can he and Cas escape in time to avenge Arnold's murder and so win their final battle with the Deadheads?

*Available Summer 1998*

## About the Author

Roy Apps began his career writing jokes for comedy programmes on radio and television. For four years he wrote for the long-running children's drama series, *Byker Grove*. Most recently, he created and wrote the children's comedy musical series *No Sweat* for the BBC.

He won the Writers' Guild Children's Book Award and was shortlisted for the Whitbread Award.

Roy regularly visits schools, libraries and bookshops to read his stories and talk about his work. He has been Writer-in-Residence at the Connaught Theatre, Worthing and has appeared at the Brighton Festival, the Kent Literature Festival and the Northern Children's Book Festival.

For more information about Roy Apps contact: The Sales Department, Macdonald Young Books, 61 Western Road, Hove, East Sussex, BN3 1JD.